PENTHOUSE F

PENTHOUSE F

RICHARD KALICH

GREEN INTEGER
KØBENHAVN & LOS ANGELES
2011

GREEN INTEGER
Edited by Per Bregne
København / Los Angeles
Distributed in the United States by Consortium Book
Sales and Distribution/Perseus
Distributed in England and throughout Europe by
Turnaround Publisher Services
Unit 3, Olympia Trading Estate
Coburg Road, Wood Green, London N22 6TZ
44 (0)20 88293009

(323) 857-1115 / http://www.greeninteger.com
Green Integer
6022 Wilshire Boulevard, Suite 200A
Los Angeles, California 90036 USA

First Green Integer Edition 2011
English language translation ©2011 by Richard Kalich
Back cover material ©2011 by Green Integer
All rights reserved

Series Design: Per Bregne
Book Design and Typography: Erin Horwarth
Cover Design and Typography: Rebecca Chamlee
Cover photo: Richard Kalich

LIBRARY OF CONGRESS IN PUBLICATION DATA
Richard Kalich (1947)
Penthouse F
ISBN: 978-1-55713-413-4
p. cm – Green Integer 179
I. Title II. Series
Green Integer books are published for Douglas Messerli
Printed in the United States of America on acid-free paper.

For My "First" favorite nephew,
George Knute Broady

"I'm nothing. I'll always be nothing. I can't want to be something. But I have in me all the dreams of the world."

— *The Book of Disquiet*
Fernando Pessoa

3/18/81 || NOTES ||

TRANSFIGURATION OF THE COMMONPLACE

Haberman—

Haberman and his two young friends are found dead in Haberan's apartment. Why? What happened? A writer is fascinated by the small commentary in the newspaper. He investigates and werit writes his version/interpretation of the expereince.

Now published and a best seller he tells the world in an interview on Sixty minutes with a live audience in front of him the story. How and whyh he wrote it. How he strated with no more than scraps of information about the deceasd; video tappes and notes and ideas ana anecdotes and comments from people who know Habemran. What he gathers and translates; garners and interprets; makes comment on and takes off on: is our story. A story novelistic rendition of The Interview; of one man's dealing with today's world...The audinece c

The tv audience is alos more interested in the images and crane their necks rather than lsiten to the writer's words. The vidoe comaera as modern day mirror of our unreal lives, diaphonous lives.

It reads or could read like a Trial; an Interview; an criminal investigation of the guilty and condemned; of the writer's culpability; there is rumour he is Haberman; taht he invented the entire scheme; idea; got notoritety. a tv program has is being modeled after the event and people all over theworld now ahve picked up on the idea and have closeted their own boys and girls and rendered haberrman's alternative lifestyle to become their own. Something has to be donwe andfor that reason the Interview has been scheduled by a reluctant writer, producer; publisher; not looking for chaeap and inflamatory publicity...or are they? Commercial world; real world with real every day considerations. (nice irony).

(copy of 76)

****Maybe the book has influenced a 'plaxgue' of simu-
lators to Haberman's alternative lifestyle. An idea whose
time has come; a rash of Haberman's have been ignited and
the writerr who created fiction from his initial inspiration
is now asked to be interviewed to haflp explain the contempora5ry
crisis; events, plaxgue, of MOBERN MAN. He is cordial and
dry, ironic and knowledgeable, but mostly he himself is prone
and fretful of the same malady as his character...he cannot
get himelef to merely articulate, explain, cmake bold comment
on something he, we all suffer and endure and lsoe out to
more and more every day. He finds himself becomeing more
increasingly like Haberman. He himself had a penchant, a
prediclection, to beocme Haberman. Why That's why why th-
stroy interested him in the first place. Maybe he is Haberman
the writer and character are one. The point is everythij-g
in our world today stands up to criss; to unreality; to
interpretation. Teh Vidoe cmaaer and image are the transmogrifier
of reality. NO one's home. Wcare literally able? from
our own sheumt. We are albert...

TRANSFIGURATION OF THE COMMONPLACE

Haberman either confesses or ~~professes guilt or explains himself to a judge, jury, tv audience,~~ and those entities, that 'YOU' like in The Fall is ourselves. Haberman addresses his court. the court in his own mind, they, we, you, them, us, he, evryone has led him to do waht he has done. The producer who saw his opportunity vurtually sought Haberman out: ~~loved idea~~ loved Habermans's idea even before the words were out of his mouth, saw it's potential, understood its potential to excite and attract even before Habemran himself understood it the fullest implicatons of waht his diea meant and would mean to his audience. at large. But of course what did Habemran know of markets and television. He was just one man, a simple man with a penchamg for writeing: he was / in a sense following his instincts, himself, no more and no less. He had no diea at last in the beginning, what he was getting into The idea just evolved on its own. It started out harmless enough and the then the rest took over. ~~Who is What is~~ the rest? asks the Prosecutior. and ~~Aalll~~ eyes and ears lean forward. Them says Haberan. The producer the executives who make descisions and ultimateslv the audience, the audience. They all loved my show.

Yes this could be the way to do it. HAVE FUN...We are all Haberman and the tv audience is our metaphor ~~bot h~~ in the programming, h½BEMRAN'S PROGRAMMING AND ITS AUDIENCE...The audience i_____ is responsible for the program much like Habemrn...We all invent ~~ou~~ ~~what~~ we see Blur the distinctions of reality..The idea of the produce℃ is to affect as much REALITY as possibne. Thus ~~he saw~~ at once taht Haberman as creator, inspirtaion, subject, and writer, was perfect. No more ~~or a~~ eloquent spokesman could he find. "It was a stroke of luck, ~~the~~ ~~lu~~ckiest day in my li¼fe when this man walk,ed into my offcie with such an idea."

The day of Hab erman 's retirement, 3/18/92...the day he puts his last bok book down, underlined, no more books, from now on Habemran will live...life to the fullest.

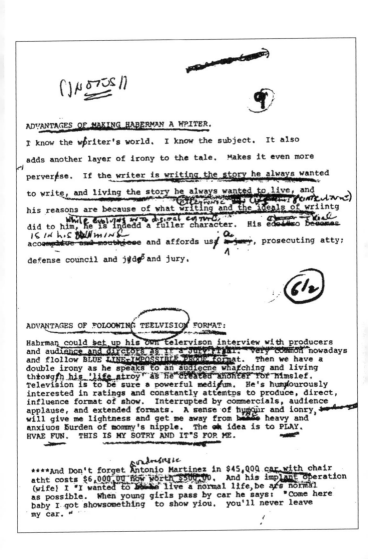

(12/20/11)

9

ADVANTAGES OF MAKING HABERMAN A WRITER.

I know the writer's world. I know the subject. It also

adds another layer of irony to the tale. Makes it even more

perverse. If the writer is writing the story he always wanted

to write, and living the story he always wanted to live, and

his reasons are because of what writing and the ideals of wriintg

did to him, he is indedd a fuller character. His ego also becomes

accomplice and mouthieec and affords us a jury, prosecuting atty;

defense council and judge and jury.

6/2

ADVANTAGES OF FOLOOWING TEELVISION FORMAT:

Habrman could set up his own telervison interview with producers
and audience and dirctors as if a jury trial. Very common nowadays
and flollow BLUE LINE.IMPOSSIBLE PROOF format. Then we have a
double irony as he speaks to an audiecne whatching and living
throughh his 'life stroy' as he created another for himslef.
Television is to be sure a powerful medigum. He's hum=ourously
interested in ratings and constantly attemtps to produce, direct,
influence format of show. Interrupted by commercials, audience
applause, and extended formats. A sense of humour and ionry,
will give me lightness and get me away from heavy and
anxiuos burden of mommy's nipple. The oh idea is to PLAY.
HVAE FUN. THIS IS MY SOTRY AND IT'S FOR ME.

****And Don't forget Antonio Martinez in $45,000 car with chair
atht costs $6,000.00 now worth $500.00. And his implant operation
(wife) I "I wanted to live a normal life, be as normal
as possible. When young girls pass by car he says: "Come here
baby I got showsomething to show yiou. you'll never leave
my car. "

7/10/8? //notes A

Agenda: More and more I like the idea and seem to be leaning
toward the idea of putting Habemran on trial in a tv version
where his producer and audience and cameraman surround him and he
has center stage a nswring questions from the audience as well as
call-ins from the aduence in the theater and the nation at large.
This could be in his head, ~~xxxxxxxxxxxxxxxxx~~, or realistically
protrayed. He can then tell his story and weave the plot in too.
Also it gives me the cahnce to psychologize and off affords me the
samee freedom was the OPEN ~~open~~ novel. And the form is ~~xxxxx and~~
approppiyte. A ~~xx~~ novel on the electronics age parodving the ao
age by its form.

6/18/05 - Anticipated Reality TV age in (1981)

NOTES:

****The more I include the READER in the GAME; the VIEWER
     in the PROGRAM (story), allow them to participate in
     the Questions and Answers...the better.

****And by using a TRIAL I can "PLAY" with the READER as
     a "PARTICIPANT."...As PLAYING IN THE GAME.

- You are the Writer, Richard Kalich.

- I could never say that with any degree of certainty. Besides, isn't that one of the reasons why we're here? To establish who I am?

- But this is your manuscript, is it not? Found in a hidden-away recess in your closet. In your apartment: PH-F.

- Hardly a manuscript: More like notes, ideas, quotes and tidbits accumulated over the years. What's the date on the first page...March 18, 1981?

- I realize some time has passed. Much has happened. But it's your handwriting. That much you'll admit: Won't you?

- Again, as I've told you countless times already. It's more like scribblings and chicken scratches.

- MR. KALICH. MR. KALICH. I WANT YOU TO TAKE WHAT I SAY SERIOUSLY...

- AND NOT SERIOUSLY AT ALL.

- You were in the park at the time of the boy and girl's suicide?

- I've already said that countless times, too.

- But it's a well-known fact that you rarely, if ever, go to the park alone.

- But this time I did. You can ask those people I spoke to and acknowledged in the park. Ask Fernando, the doorman.

- We already did.

- Well, the point is, I wasn't there when they jumped off the terrace. I had nothing to do with the children's decision to...

- It's not that simple, Mr. Kalich.

I came up with the idea for the novel, "The Transfiguration of the Commonplace," almost twenty-five years ago; but I could never really write it. Creative block, call it what you will, the fact is I remained obsessed with it until the boy and girl came into my life. Although, to be sure, they were the main characters in my would-be novel, too.

"Could I ever really write at random and without design, thus glimpsing the chaos, the disorder of my own depths?"

—Tommaso Landolfi

Constipation (kon'sta pa' shan), n. 1. a condition of the bowels in which the feces are dry and hardened and evacuation is difficult and infrequent. 2. Obs. the act of crowding anything into a smaller compass; condensation. (ME *constipacioun* = LL constipation-s. of *constipatio*.) See CONSTIPATE. –ION

Through most of my life I have been constipated. Sometimes there were months and even more that I didn't defecate and then, finally, when I did, the feces was so large and hardened I had to cut it into smaller sections in order to let it flush down the toilet. The problem lasted well into my forties and early fifties. Today, at this belated stage in my life, I am happy to report I am what is commonly referred to as "regular."

When I am seated before the TV monitor observing the boy and girl, somehow all seems different. The boy and girl, though very much flesh and blood, real, take on another dimension. I, myself, am different. At those times, seated or standing before the screen, observing, watching the boy and girl, I am...how do I say this...more alive than they. In charge. They, like puppets on a string, seemingly anticipate my every command.

- When you returned from the park that ever fateful day and saw the police cars, and EMR ambulance and yellow tape cordoning off the covered bodies from the crowd--why did you not ask what happened?

- I already knew.

- How did you already know?

- I just did. The pool of blood. All that hubbub and confusion. It was obvious somebody had leaped to their death. Who else could it be but them?

- And the aborted notes in your novel say as much. Do they not?

- It's not the same thing.

- I agree. Writing fiction is not life.

- It's not that simple.

When I was writing my novel, or at least jotting down notes in preparation, I had no one to answer to but myself. I could let my imagination take me where it would.

- Nothing is simple, Mr. Kalich.

But once I arranged for the boy and girl to enter my life, commenced choreographing their plottings in earnest, there was something inaugural and new about it. All was different.

- Least of all differentiating your fictions from what is real.

In the middle of the night, when I wake to scribble down ideas in a notebook lying close to my bed, I never turn the lights on. It is pitch black. I prefer it that way. To be alone with my imagination. Watching the boy and girl on screen, I become increasingly frustrated when they move into the shadows. If I could, I would have them take center stage and remain in the spotlight for the duration.

> - Again I must ask: Why on that particular
> day did you go to the park alone? You, who
> has not been seen in the park alone once
> since the boy and girl took up residence
> in your apartment. And I might also add:
> You, who has not taken a vacation, left
> the city, visited a friend or a neighbor,
> nobody, nothing, why then, that day, did
> you decide to leave the boy and girl and
> go to the park alone?

I stand silent not giving the Interrogator the satisfaction
of an answer.

> - You can see we know your habits, Mr.
> Kalich. We know, for example, the last
> time you took as much as a semblance of
> a vacation was when you travelled out
> of the country more than thirty years
> ago, September 1978 to be precise, to
> the Frankfurt Book Fair, to celebrate
> the publication of your first novel "The
> Nihilesthete." It does no good to deny
> these facts, Mr. Kalich. The building
> staff and various residents in the
> building have attested as much.

Not that I have a satisfactory answer for myself.

Please don't get the idea that just because I was behind the camera, so to speak, and the boy and girl were on stage, so to speak, that it was all fun and games for me. Admittedly it was that, in fact, merely getting away from writing that book was of the profoundest relief. A joy I had not experienced in years. But still, in all honesty, in the beginning, fun and games might be construed as my primary motive.

    - Once you put down your pen and pencil on
    your would-be novel...

    - I use an old IBM Selectric.

    - ...you immediately set upon a new course
    of action.

    - It came to me in a moment of insight. I
    knew what I had to do.

    - Not hardly a moment of insight, Mr.
    Kalich, more like over a period of time.
    With careful deliberation and more than a
    little calculation and cunning.

I remain silent.

    - Well then, how do you explain
    rearranging your apartment to accommodate

the boy and girl in exactly the same
manner as you so painstakingly depicted in
your notes for the novel?

- How else would I arrange it? Once I
realized what I must do, and as I say,
it came to me like a belated moment of
inspiration, of course I relied on what
was tried and true. Familiar. I won't deny
I was obsessed with the boy and girl for
years. We both know that much. It's all
there in black and white.

- The difference is, and I ask this not
merely out of curiosity, Mr. Kalich, whatever
possessed you to think you could live the
experience you so painstakingly made such
Promethean efforts to write about and failed?

- You said it yourself.

- And what did I say?

- I failed.

The two things I had the most capacity for in my life, loving a woman and writing, terrified me most. Though in
different ways, I ran from each with equal fervor.

When I came up with the idea for the novel, "The Transfiguration of the Commonplace," like all my other novels, I saw it whole, a poetic image, a central metaphor. In this case, my main character, Haberman, would be the same character that was in my first novel, "The Nihilesthete;" but this time watching, observing, choreographing the boy and girl's behavior on a TV monitor. I remember being so excited that I called up my various publishers and agents, Marion Boyars in England, Svetlana Paccher in France, Martin Shepherd in Sag Harbor, as well as my twin brother, to tell them that I had the definitive novel of our time. I actually said that. The novel anticipated the virtual reality revolution. When I first conceived the novel there was no such thing as a desktop/personal computer, virtual reality, the image supplanting the word.

- You've been employed as a cleaning lady by Mr. Kalich for more than twenty years.

- I was a Professor of Mathematics in Poland before I came to the United States.

- And now, in this last year or so, since the boy and girl came to reside, you say you've seen great changes in Mr. Kalich.

- For Mr. Kalich they were great.

- Can you describe some of these "great" changes?

- For one, Mr. Kalich asked that I clean the apartment at least once a week. Before the boy and girl...

Marta giggles to herself.

- ...it might have been no more than once or twice every three months. When I came to clean, the apartment would be knee-deep in clutter, books and paper lying about everywhere, filth and dustballs. I would have to scrub until my fingers were raw. I would leave exhausted.

- And that included the boy and girl's respective rooms?

- Oh, no, Mr. Kalich was very clear on that. I was not to enter those rooms for any reason.

- How do you account for that?

- I suppose he wanted the boy and girl to learn to assume their own responsibilities.

- Like a strict and stern parent.

- I didn't mean it like that.

- How did you mean it?

- Like a good parent.

I wrote my first novel at the age of twenty-six. I should say my first effort. A study in futility. My twin brother said it was the worst piece of literary constipation he had ever read. I blame two people. My mother: a European banker's daughter who lovingly announced to her children: I want scholars and artists, poets and writers, for sons. Not businessmen. Never businessmen. Translated: I had to be Dostoevski or nothing. And Thomas Mann. The reason my first novel was "the worst piece of literary constipation" was that I was so enamored or rather reverential of the great Mann that I attempted to emulate if not simulate his ornate old German prose.

It cost me another fifteen to twenty years before I could break free of such matriarchal and patriarchal orthodoxies and find my own voice.

- What other changes came over Mr. Kalich, Marta, since the boy and girl arrived?

- He smiled more.

Marta smiles.

- Because of the boy and girl?

- He was happy.

- And...?

- He dressed better. You know, snappy. Like young people do nowadays. In fact I used to tease him that since their arrival he looks years younger. I wasn't the only one who said that.

- But you never once entered their rooms?

- I already told you that. No.

The most interesting aspect in the course of my writing the notes and collecting insights and material for the novel was how little by little, day by day, week by week, over months and years, the various newspapers, media, magazines, literary quarterlies and scholarly journals, would make comment, small at first, a mere paragraph or two,

then larger, a full page, and larger, regardi
reality phenomena; the computer, the detr
ence of television: Make comments on jus
had intuited poetically and was preparing to dramat...
my novel.

In March, 1981 I had conceived my novel, had seen it whole. By 1989 there had already been a film out, a mere trifling compared to what I had in mind for my novel: a comic book: a shallow and superficial dramaturgy, but yet it received much acclaim. It wasn't long before I felt my time had passed. No matter what I might create, no matter how profound, brilliant or ambitious, I felt I would never again gain credit for being the first.

(Grandiosity has always been my downfall.)

But still, I knew I had to write my novel. But, of course, I could not.

> "Seeing is no longer believing. The very notion of truth and how it manifests itself in pictures and words has been put into crisis. In a world bloated with images, we are finally learning that photographs do indeed lie. In a society rife with purported information, we know that words have power but usually they don't mean anything. To

put it bluntly, no one's home. We are elsewhere, not in the real world but in the represented. Our bodies, the flesh and blood of it all, have given way to representations: figures that cavort on TV, movie and computer screens. Propped up and ultra-relaxed, we teeter on the cusp of narcolepsy and believe in everything and nothing."

—*NY Times,* Sept. 10, 1990,
Barbara Kruger

Every novelist has one novel in him. The rest are mere variations on the theme.

"Transfiguration of the Commonplace" was my one novel.

- Isn't it peculiar, Mr. Kalich, that on the very day you decided to take a walk in Central Park alone, during those very same hours, the boy and girl likewise decided to leave the apartment? Something they very rarely, if ever, did.

- That's why I went for a walk in the park alone.

- But the boy and girl weren't alone. They were together.

- Yes. They had tickets for the theater.

- Which you purchased for them, Mr. Kalich. "Romeo and Juliet" if I'm not mistaken.

When I graduated City College in 1959 I remember standing on the steps of Townsend Hall telling three or four other graduates: "I don't know what I'm going to do with my life, but one thing I do know: I'll never go into business."

- Three hours! You spent three hours on that Sunday of the boy and girl's suicide listening to David Ippolito, otherwise known as "The Guitar Man of Central Park," sing his songs.

- It's really the most beautiful location in the park, there on the hill overlooking the lake, people rowing, ducks paddling near the shore.

- But three hours, Mr. Kalich. For a man who is reputedly tone deaf.

- I wouldn't say that.

- We have it on good account from more
than several people, including the
harpist, Dobrinka Nacheva, that you were
no great lover of music. In fact for the
four years the harpist was in your life
you rarely if ever attended any of her
concerts.

- The boy and girl got me in the habit
of going to the park every Sunday. It
became a kind of ritual for us. They loved
Ippolito's music.

- But that's just the point, Mr. Kalich.
On this particular Sunday the boy and girl
were not with you. You attended alone.

I remain silent.

- And in those three hours, I venture,
and this is not a guess, Mr. Kalich, Mr.
Ippolito had time enough to sing his
entire repertoire, some eighty-five to one
hundred songs. Can you recall any of the
songs?

Just a twitch of my mouth.

- No.

- Three hours! Eighty-five to one hundred
songs! And you cannot recollect even one
song?! That seems strange. Perhaps you
weren't really listening. Would it be fair
to surmise that you had other things on
your mind?

At the time I graduated City College, or perhaps one or
two months earlier, I made myself a promise: I would read
ten pages of the greatest minds in the world every day for
the rest of my life. To be accurate: Ten or more pages.

Other than those three or four times I was working on a
novel, I kept my promise.

- Scary.

- Scary?

- Scary. That was the title of one of his
songs.

- Really...

- Tom Cruise is scary. Oprah is scary.
Dick Cheney is scary. Really quite a
clever and amusing lyric don't you think?

- Undoubtedly. But after that song which
Ippolito sang at exactly 3:00 p.m., our
reports indicate you rushed off. Why then?
Why at that precise time? As if you had
an appointment or perhaps something more
urgent was pressing.

I remain silent.

- Interesting, is it not: Of the
eighty-five to one hundred songs in the
guitarist's repertoire, the one title you
remember is titled "Scary."

- Five o'clock is the time matinees
usually break on Sundays. Even I know that
much. I left early because of the rain.

- The question, Mr. Kalich, is: Is that
all you knew?

It would be a mistake to assume that I sought out and
invited the boy and girl into my apartment just because
I could not write my novel; because I wanted to rid myself of the terror of creation by diverting myself with some
kind of entertainment. A game perhaps. No. Never was I
merely a game-player: never was it merely a matter of winning and losing. What caught hold of me in that epiphanic

30

moment was the game itself. The idea that the boy and girl, those imagined fictionalized characters which I had obsessed over for so long and could not release from the fecundity of my unconscious onto the written page, would now be able to make themselves manifest in everyday reality. After all, staging, programming and conjuring up scene by scene episodes for flesh and blood reality, live action dramaturgy, is really not that different than imagining, constructing and wrenching forth plot points for a book. Real or imagined, game or novel, one aspect remained the same: It lay within my powers to dictate the way the game would be played. At long last the boy and girl, my two imagined characters, would become real.

To be sure there were deeper more complex motives spurring me on as well. From the fetid impotence of my failed writer's powerlessness, I would now, for the first time since my dream-laden youth, know something of the long lost "Authority" of earlier century writers. Also, there was the added attraction of giving my writer's imagination, so long bursting at the seams over stillborn and vainglorious waters, the chance to unburden itself. To give vent and full glory to all that lay buried inside me. If I could not realize and complete myself with the written word, why not on stage and screen with live-action flesh and blood human beings.

- You are James McDonough.

- That's my name.

- You were an elevator operator in Mr. Kalich's building for thirty-seven years.

- Not always an elevator operator. I was transferred to the front desk when the building put in a self-service elevator.

- But it would be fair to say you knew Mr. Kalich well.

- For sure. He moved into PH-F three years after I started in 1965.

- How would you describe Mr. Kalich?

I remember sitting at the typewriter with two novels in me. "The Nihilesthete" and "The Zoo." For two days I attempted mightily to wrench the first words out for "The Nihilesthete." Not a word. Sentence. Paragraph. Nothing. Blank pages. Zilch. On the third day I decided to change over and make an effort to write "The Zoo." Behold: a miracle. In thirty days I had my first draft.

- What kind of person is Mr. Kalich, Mr. McDonough?

- I can't say. That's not an easy question to answer.

- Why is the question not easy?

- Because Mr. Kalich was two different people. For years, when young, he was one person; then later, when he got older, another.

Who can account for miracles?

- What were the differences, Mr. McDonough? For example, when Mr. Kalich was young, how was he?

- He read books and wrote books.

- And later...

- For years I never once saw Mr. Kalich leave the building without a book in his hand.

Dr. Lawrence Katt could. A psychiatrist who specialized in artist's maladies and disorders. Now that my twin brother had written and published his novel, he said, I would be able to write mine. With twins it was chicken and egg, he said. First one, then the other.

- And when he got older, Mr. McDonough?

- He no longer carried books.

- Did his personality change as well?

- I don't understand the question.

- Was he seemingly more troubled, dour, moody, depressed, angry?

- I don't know about that, but...

- But...?

- He kind of lost something. He wasn't there.

- Could you elaborate, Mr. McDonough?

- The old Mr. Kalich disappeared. He became like everybody else.

- Please be specific, Mr. McDonough. Cite an example.

- He became silent. He stopped talking to people. Didn't say a word to the other tenants and not much more to us, the staff, except, maybe, when passing through the lobby.

- And what did Mr. Kalich say to the staff when passing through the lobby?

- Nothing much. You know. Hi, take care, the usual. Most of the time he would just speak out our names. Fernando. James. Pastor. Big George.

- In the later years leading up to your retirement, did Mr. Kalich cause any problems in the building? Would you, for example, say he was a problem tenant?

- Oh, no. Mr. Kalich wasn't like that. He was never a troublemaker like 9G. That one would come home drunk every night, with a different woman, if you catch my drift. He would beat them up, too. We had to call the police more than once. No fooling.

- And Mr. Kalich?

- I can tell you stories about people
in this building you wouldn't believe.
Bankers, lawyers, celebrities, especially
celebrities. One time we had an
assemblyman living here and he would have
his gay lovers sneak up to his apartment
only after midnight so none of the other
tenants would see them.

- Can you tell us any stories specifically
about Mr. Kalich?

Mr. McDonough shakes his head. No.

- Even after the boy and girl moved into
PH-F?

- I don't know. I was only there a few
weeks after they moved in.

- Can you tell us anything about those few
weeks?

- As I said. Those last years, when Mr.
Kalich got older, he disappeared.

Arranging, decorating, preparing rooms for a boy and girl was one thing. Selecting the boy and girl another. One can't just pick a boy and girl out of a store window like a stick of furniture and expect to know what one is getting. And even if my assiduous notes told me what qualities in the boy and girl to look for in a literary and psychological sense, I very well understood that there was more to an actual, real-life boy and girl than I could ever have envisioned in my imagination or written on the page.

- You are Terrance Kearney, Mr. Kalich's neighbor.

- Next door neighbor, actually. We've shared the two apartments on the penthouse floor for at least ten years.

- Eleven years and six months to be precise.

- Of course I own my apartment. Mr. Kalich's penthouse F is rent-controlled. Lucky stiff.

- Mr. Kearney. You are employed at the Parke Bernet Galleries selling fine paintings and artifacts of antiquity since graduating Princeton in 1994.

- Yes. What's your point?

- I would think you and Mr. Kalich have much in common. Have developed a good and solid friendship over the years, both of you being involved in the arts in one way or another.

- No. Not really. Other than bumping into each other in the hallway when trashing our garbage, or sharing the elevator when leaving or maybe coming home, we've probably never said more than a half dozen words to each other.

- Why is that?

- At most he might have recommended a movie he had just seen at the arthouse theater on 63rd Street and Broadway.

- Is Mr. Kalich so antisocial?

- Not only that. But as you must know, we have different sexual orientations.

Regarding the Selection Process for the boy and girl, there were more than several qualities that I deemed prerequisite. Qualities and characteristics that I could not do without. For one the boy and girl could not be particularly perceptive. Nor strong-willed. Certainly not self-reliant. Possessing any of those qualities would have disqualified them immediately.

    - And Mr. Kalich held that against you?

    - It never came up. That's not what I
    meant to infer. It's just that we went our
    own ways, I had my life and he had his.

My neighbor and his friends comprised a close-knit community, all different, all the same; they would come together once a week, on Friday nights. There was always much laughter, bacchanalian yelling and singing, and music. Loud music. The next morning the garbage cans in the alcove by the service elevator would be spilling over with champagne bottles and beer cans.

    - In fact it was a standard joke between
    us. Mr. Kalich would quip that maybe he
    should become gay. That his social life
    would be far better if he was.

A writer starts out with an idea for a novel and commences to lead his characters along the way. It's not long before the characters are leading the writer. Sooner than not the writer is merely taking dictation. I could not afford that to happen with the boy and girl. This was not merely another would-be novel I was planning to write.

- Mr. Kearney, a moment ago you said that you and Mr. Kalich never spoke more than a few words to each other. Next you make mention of his recommending films for you to see. And now you speak of his sharing quips and jokes with you. You can't have it all ways, Mr. Kearney.

- You misunderstand me. In ten... eleven years, there's always those few exceptions. Of course there was also that one time.

- One time?

- Yes. I was living with an investment banker friend. We had both made a good sum of money that year, as I had taken advantage of his tips and suggestions in the market, and we decided to make Mr. Kalich an offer to purchase his apartment. Adding his four rooms

to our two would have been a real coup. If
he agreed, I knew I could work something out
with the building's management.

- Obviously he rejected your offer.

- Yes. At any rate we were both standing
on our terraces, actually Mr. Kalich was
in his doorway leading out to the terrace.
And we started to talk. I broached the
subject and, then, when it started to
rain, we continued our conversation in
his apartment. It was the only time I can
recall ever being in his apartment.

- As I said. You weren't successful in
persuading Mr. Kalich to sell.

- No. He was very much against it. But it
was the way he rejected my proposal that
stays in my mind. What he said...

- And what was that?

- He said PH-F, with its view overlooking
Central Park, was the one luxury he had in
all the world. It wasn't so much what he
said, as the way he said it.

More important than all the rest was that the boy and girl must be pathologically in need of love. This need has to be central to their makeup. It would be ideal if, for one reason or another, they had been denied contact with the opposite sex in their adolescent years. Even better, all their lives. I needed them to hunger for intimacy without, if possible, either of them even realizing it.

- Of course that was before the boy and girl moved in.

- And when the boy and girl moved in?

- He seemed to lighten up overnight.

- And the boy and girl. Can you tell us what went on between Mr. Kalich and the boy and girl in PH- F?

- Who knows what went on there.

- How is that possible? They, at least for a certain period of time, were as much your next door neighbors as Mr. Kalich was.

- I hardly ever saw them. And, if I did, passing through the lobby or waiting for the elevator, they would avert their eyes. I don't

42

recall them ever looking me in the eye. And if
they spotted me first, say in the hallway, or
lobby, they would scamper off like squirrels
up a tree. I always thought they were hiding
something. They certainly acted strange.

- Was anything else...strange? This is
extremely important, Mr. Kearney.

Mr. Kearney shakes his head.

- No.

- Anything. The slightest detail could be
crucial.

- Well, there is one thing.

- Yes?

- Nothing much, just the fact that the
last several months before their suicide,
PH-F seemed awfully quiet.

- Was it noisy before?

- No, but more than once I would hear
shouting and arguments going on.

```
- Can you tell us anything about those
arguments and shouting going on between
Mr. Kalich and the boy and girl?

- No sir, I cannot. I'm no eavesdropper.
```

When was it that I stopped reading books?

*"My body is tired. Alas! And I've read all the
books."*

— Mallarmé

I do know it was long before the boy and girl arrived.

```
- Marta, why is it that you failed to
mention the many shouting matches and
arguments that occurred between Mr. Kalich
and the boy and girl those last several
months prior to their suicide?

- I didn't think it was important.

- How could it not be important, Marta?
The boy and girl literally leaped to their
```

death from the man's terrace. We have to
assume someone or something provoked such
an action.

- All close families have fights and
arguments between them. Then they kiss and
make up. It's only normal.

When I am observing the boy and girl on my TV monitor from the little TV room secretly hidden away inside
my closet, a feeling of levity and lightheartedness always
comes over me; at least for much of that first year. I felt
as if I was entering a new chapter in my life. A chapter as
lighthearted as a game. Looking back I realize now I have
my twin's three-year-old son, Knute, to thank for this
miraculous transformation of self. Periodically my brother would ask me to babysit (which was not very often,
thankfully—after twenty minutes I was exhausted and
started to count the minutes to my twin and his wife's return) and almost immediately after his parent's departure,
the three-year-old would commence climbing down from
his bed, scrutinize with knitted brows his great collection
of toys and games, scrupulously select one, then, taking me by the hand into the larger, more spacious living
room, he would say: "Let's play." Not that I would join in,
but I would watch in utter amazement as the boy would

explore, invent, create and discover meaning where just before there was only chaos. Not withstanding the good doctor's chicken and egg interpretation, my epiphany took place in just those moments.

In other words, I knew I had found my way.

- So, Mr. Kalich, we have established that after spending at least one month or more scouring the Upper West Side city streets for such a pair: placing ads to sublet rooms in your apartment in several newspapers; on neighborhood storefronts and bulletin boards; frequenting young people's clubs and hangouts; you finally commenced concentrating your efforts in an old halfway house in East Harlem.

- Yes. I had had peripheral association with the halfway house when I was employed as a case worker for the Department of Social Services.

- You were employed by the Department of Social Services for twenty-nine years, and left upon reaching the retirement age of fifty-five. Were you not?

- I would only add I hated every minute, day and hour I worked for the Department.

- According to our records, you visited the halfway house in the capacity of a volunteer worker three to four times a week, for a period spanning at least three months. You were friendly with the Director.

- Rather than friendship, I would say we shared mutual sympathies.

- And I have to assume, despite your self-professed hatred of social work, this volunteer work facilitated your search for the proper boy and girl?

- Once the Director knew what I was looking for, of course he didn't really know, I could not very well explain the full subtleties and complexities of the personalities I desired. At the time I hardly knew myself. But still, after I studied his casework files I had a much better idea as to which boys and girls might meet my needs.

- And out of some thirty-five to fifty residents you were able to decide on these particular two.

- Yes. Peculiar thing is, though, that I had seen them on the street panhandling together near my building more than once before and never noticed them. It was as if they weren't there.

- And yet in the halfway house you did notice them?

- Yes.

- Why was that?

- I don't know. I guess they just seemed to be in the proper setting. Like pictures in a frame.

- Or perhaps, might I suggest: images on a screen?

- If you must.

- But still, Mr. Kalich, I must ask you to elaborate further.

- As I said it's not easy to explain. The young woman, for example, she was no more than seventeen, eighteen. What stood

out first and foremost about her was her
physical beauty, her candle-colored skin,
but that's hardly the point.

- What was the point, Mr. Kalich?

- Well, she had a childhood history of
aphasia which I found interesting; but
more interesting to me was the fact that
she, like so many others from her world,
had been molested by her stepfather at
a very young age and seemingly never
recovered. Additionally interesting was
that her mother was regularly seated
just outside the room while her husband
was molesting the girl and not once did
she even try to prevent it. And most
interesting of all was that in addition
to the horrific bit of trauma, or maybe
because of it, she had never experienced
intimacy with a man.

- Again, very much like you depict in your
notes for your novel.

- Yes. With one great difference though.

- And what is that great difference?

- This young woman seemed to understand what she was missing.

- And the boy?

- He was not as simple to decide upon. In fact, other than being out on the streets since he was eleven years of age, I had little to go on other than the way he gazed at the girl.

- And how was that?

- He couldn't take his eyes off her.

- That's it?!

- One other thing. Whenever the situation called for it, he would make an effort to protect her, comfort her. And even more to the point, indeed essential for my purposes, he couldn't take his hands off her even if it was no more than a brush of his fingertips against her elbow to direct her into a chair or a room.

- And on that you made your determination to rent two rooms of your precious Penthouse F to them for a ridiculously

modest sum I might add, virtually no rent
at all.

- It was hardly money I wanted from such
a pair.

- And what was it you wanted?

- I wanted to help.

When the boy and girl moved in that first night I realized
I was more in debt to the Director than I had ever let on
to my Interrogator. For when the boy gently attempted to
take the girl by her elbow to guide her through the corridor to her room, almost instantly she pulled back. Not
unlike how one might pull back one's fingers from a hot
flame. The boy was caught unawares. I was not.

With the investigation well under way at this point, one
has to ask oneself the following: What have I learned about
myself, about the boy and girl's suicide, that I didn't already know? Well, for one, I know that in my earlier years
I was a lover of books, a man of letters, a Writer, and as
the years progressed, my interest in the literary life waned.
I lost my moorings. And also I know that I invited and
welcomed the boy and girl into my home, PH-F, because
I wanted to help them, offer them succor and warmth, or

maybe it was just a matter of my being lonely, or perhaps I wanted to amuse myself, play games in one way or another. More than likely all three motives, in one combination or another, have merit. Who can say with any degree of certainty; everything is still very much open to interpretation. In fact, if I am to be completely honest, I am really no closer to knowing myself now, or understanding what transpired between myself and the boy and girl, than I was prior to when the interrogation began.

What has not been said is that though I never laid hands on either the boy or girl, when watching them on the TV monitor, viewing them in different locations in the apartment, or in their rooms, alone or together, the boy and girl seemed more real to me than anything or anybody else in my life. It was as if my hands were guiding them to wherever they might go. This must be something akin to the feeling one gets when changing channels with the remote.

```
- You were at the front desk, Mr.
Calderon, on that Sunday the boy and girl
left for the theater.

- Yes. I worked the 8 to 4 p.m. shift, but
I was off by the time they returned.
```

Perhaps it is due to what seemingly happens to them when on screen. For obvious reasons they appear smaller, but it is more than that. They are also seemingly more malleable, less willful, more like puppets in the hands of an all-powerful puppeteer. It is at those times I feel I can manipulate and maneuver, push and prod them; I feel like a writer again, like a choreographer, director, their Creator who can lead them anywhere I want.

```
- And you did not leave your station?

- No. Never.

- Maybe you had to go to the toilet or
took a smoke break.

- I told you, never.

- Never? Not one time?!

- At most I might have helped Old Man
Carmilly to the elevator. Or some mother
or nanny up the stairs to the elevator
with their baby carriages. Look. Mr.
Kalich is one of our nicest tenants.
```

- Nicest tenant?

- That's right. Other tenants talk about it, but Mr. Kalich was the only one who actually helped me with my GED exam. He read over the essay part with me and gave me books to read. Besides, if I was busy with another tenant, Big George was at the front door. And he didn't let anyone in.

Observing the boy and girl on screen in this manner, if only by the way they avert their eyes from each other, the way they avoid any and all physical contact or overt gestures of intimacy, makes me feel that it is I who am going through the time-honored rituals of courtship. Yes. The boy and girl have opened me to a whole new aspect of myself. Something so long and deeply buried that I hardly knew it even existed in myself.

- We know for a fact, Mr. Calderon, the Samuelsons were honeymooning in Greece at that time. And their wedding presents kept arriving regularly, even on Sundays.

- You're right. I forgot. I had to take some wedding gifts up to 12-C one time.

54

- And what if Big George took a break at
that exact same time you were delivering
wedding presents to the Samuelsons 12-C
apartment? What happens then?

- Big George would lock the front door so
nobody could get in.

Thanks to the boy and girl, slowly, in its own way and
time, their time and mine, I could feel myself rising to the
surface, the first blush of inner feelings coming to life.

- And if somebody wanted to enter the
building at precisely that time, would you
or Big George hear their ring?

- Not if I were delivering wedding
presents and Big George was downstairs in
the basement.

- Mr. Calderon I want you to think before
answering this next question.

The concierge prepares to think.

- Nobody was at the front door when Big
George and me returned to our stations.
But...

- But...?

- The door wasn't locked. It was open.

- Open?! Why didn't you say so before?

- I didn't want to get Big George in
trouble.

Next follows Big George.

- So it's possible, Big George, that Mr.
Kalich could have entered the building, waited
until the elevator was in service, walked up
the stairs to his penthouse apartment, and
nobody would have been the wiser.

- No, he couldn't.

- Why not?

- Because PH-F is on the top floor.
Seventeen. And Mr. Kalich is an old man.
He's got gout.

- But I thought you earlier agreed with
Mr. Calderon that since the boy and girl
entered his life, Mr. Kalich appeared

younger. He was spry...there was even a bounce to his step, you said.

- I said that?

- "You're getting younger as you get older"...those were your exact words to Mr. Kalich, Big George.

- I meant since the boy and girl moved in.

- On this matter you're also in agreement with Mr. Calderon.

- I don't know nothing. Mr. Kalich never invited me out on a date with them. At most I might have seen him and the boy and girl together in the lobby.

- What else did you notice about Mr. Kalich since the boy and girl moved in?

- Nothing. I told you already. Other than that one Sunday when I worked the front door because Fernando was sick, I was transferred to the basement with Little George. I ran the service elevator and collected the garbage on Mr. Kalich's side of the building.

- And when you took your smoke break on
that Sunday for ten to fifteen minutes, you
failed to lock the front door.

- I don't know nothing.

Notwithstanding the splattered bodies of the boy and girl
found lying on the concrete in front of my building, the
2,000 or more bones of their bodies ground to pulp, the
police forensic team documented the following: The girl
had been attired in a lace white gown and the boy in a
grey-black suit jacket and tie, as if dressed for a formal
occasion, more than likely a wedding. The girl's right
wrist was bound to the boy's left with handcuffs, those
simulated kind you can purchase in any children's toy
store. Long-stemmed champagne glasses, their contents
ostensibly drained to the last sip, were found on a small
bench-like table, and logically enough, a commensurate
amount of the bubbly white wine was likewise found in
the boy and girl's stomachs. Further forensic examination
indicated they had imbibed the wine just prior to their
plunge. One can only wonder what they were celebrating: was it real or imagined? spectacle or sham? live theater or performance art? Just as importantly, there was
no evidence of foul play; no indication that any violence,
sexual or otherwise, had been perpetrated on the pair. No

scratch marks, bruises, no skin tissue underneath their fingernails to suggest physical confrontation or any kind of a defensive battle. No. The double suicide, if nothing else, appeared wholly voluntary. And, oh yes, the boy and girl each had a playbill on their person: the boy in his right vest suit jacket pocket, the girl tied around her waist with a blue satin sash. Only to be expected, the playbills were from the matinee performance of Romeo and Juliet they had just attended only an hour or so earlier. In fact, if not on the first page, still prominently featured nevertheless, ranging from pages three to six on more than several of the next morning's newspapers, in bold black lettering, was titled: "ROMEO AND JULIET SUICIDE."

I almost hesitate to mention my immediate reaction when returning from the park and seeing the splattered bodies of the boy and girl, but in the name of accuracy, if nothing else, I must. I had the distinct feeling of completion, of somehow having finished, after a long and arduous struggle spanning over many years' battle, the last page of a novel I had been working on. Yes: All that remained for me to do was date and mark the last page, as was my habit, to bring the book to a close.

Whether shopping for groceries at the Food Emporium, having a new suit tailored at French Cleaners, or merely picking up a newspaper at the corner newsstand, I notice my step quickens as I start home.

Home...a word I never used before to describe PH-F.

For the first time in my life I have something and someone to come home for.

- Why did you purchase tickets for the boy and girl to go to the theater? And more to the point: why this particular play. Romeo and Juliet?

- I have always liked theater.

- But no longer. You gave up attending theater at the same time you stopped reading books.

- But, as you say, the tickets weren't for me. I purchased the tickets for the boy and girl.

- Exactly. So again I must ask why?

- Obviously I thought they would enjoy the play. Get something from it.

- An interesting turn of phrase, wouldn't you agree?

- What?

- "Get something from it."

- People have been enjoying and getting something from Shakespeare for centuries.

- But I would think appreciating Shakespeare is well beyond this particular boy and girl's capacities. They are, after all, both flawed. Mentally limited. We have on record that both their IQs are no more than seventy-five. That's very close to or considered a moronic level, is it not?

- They're not morons! A moron is a person having an IQ of 50-69 and judged incapable of developing beyond a mental age of eight to twelve.

- Retarded then?

    - They might be slow, somewhat retarded.

    - Slow...retarded. And yet you purchased
    tickets for them to see Shakespeare!?

Of course when I reach home I don't immediately make it
a point to visit with the boy and girl. Rather I head directly
to my TV Room to observe them.

    - You noticed Mr. Kalich and the young
    woman as soon as they entered the women's
    area on the second floor.

The sales rep nods his head.

    - Why was that?

    - A young woman and a mature gentleman
    always catch my eye. I guess it's my
    salesman's instinct. The old ones always
    spend more.

    - And that's what happened on this
    occasion?

    - As soon as the young woman asked to try
    on our white Juliet dress displayed on the

cover page of our fall brochure, I knew he
was a goner.

- The brochure with the Romeo and Juliet
thematic logo?

- That's the one.

- What do you mean when you say: Mr.
Kalich was a goner?

- Actually it was the way both of them
looked.

- Both of them?

- Well, when Mr. Kalich first saw the young
woman in the white dress, he just stood
there as if mesmerized.

- And the young woman?

- She was absolutely beautiful. Radiant.
But to be more accurate, she didn't
so much come out of the dressing room
as peeked out. Her face flushed as if
embarrassed.

- Why was she embarrassed?

- I've seen that look before. The young woman's at that awkward age, half woman, half girl. I would bet anything she was asking herself those questions young girls always ask: Do I belong here? Is this really me? You know--am I a woman or still a girl?

- And Mr. Kalich. Can you elaborate further on how he reacted when seeing the young woman first peek out of the dressing room?

- He immediately purchased the dress. I had the impression no expense would have been too great for him.

- Did you notice anything else about Mr. Kalich and the young girl?

- Well, she gave him a thank you kiss. Just a peck on the cheek, really.

- Was Mr. Kalich disappointed?

- I wouldn't say that. At least at the time I didn't think so. But a little later I changed my mind.

- What made you change your mind?

- A customer standing nearby, an elegant
lady, made a comment to Mr. Kalich saying:
"You have a beautiful daughter."

- And how did Mr. Kalich react to the
elegant lady's comment: "You have a
beautiful daughter?"

- It was an awkward moment to say the
least. But somehow he managed a polite
smile and thank you. But anyone could see
it was a forced smile.

- Did you notice anything else about Mr.
Kalich after the elegant lady's comment?

- Despite my rushing him away from the
scene of the crime, so to speak, after
paying for the dress he left the store in
a huff.

- And the girl?

- She followed after him, poor thing, like
a naughty child with her fingers caught in
the cookie jar.

- You're not exaggerating?

- No, not at all. It doesn't take much more than that to break the spell. That's why we salesmen have to be constantly on guard against eventualities like that.

- And this time you were not?

- I guess not. The woman caught me off guard. I must have been staring at the young girl as much as Mr. Kalich. As the brochure suggests. Romeo and Juliet. It's all illusion. Magic, you know. For those few seconds when the girl made her entrance out of the dressing room wearing the white dress, who can say what was in the old man's mind.

- I take it not like a doting father.

- More like a Romeo who had found his Juliet.

As if to validate, if only to himself, the sales rep nods his head.

- Mr. Kalich, you say you would have given anything to have videotaped the young girl's face when first peeking her head out of the dressing room.

- Anything.

- But why? By your own admission the moment is indelibly imprinted in your mind.

- On tape I would be able to play it over and over again, not merely in my mind, but on screen.

From that day on I was consumed by the idea of placing the girl in a comparable situation again.

"The folks in the paneled offices are beginning to play fast and loose with authenticity. There is trust in simulation—that is, in people's willingness to accept the staged experience, not because they have been made to believe in it, but because they are willing to live with a substitute, will accept it in a spirit of 'something is better than nothing.' In other words, if you can coin the feeling of a thing, replicate somehow a sense of the

experience, then, for many, you have as good as provided the real experience.

The shift, this collective willingness to go with the ersatz, has profound implications. It bears directly on the difference—and the importance of the difference—between the real and the virtual. Virtuality. Fantasy experience. Surrogate living to take the edge off our clamorous needs."

— *Readings*,
Sven Birkerts

- Mr. Kalich was never like this in the old days.

- What do you mean: the old days?

- He used to come into the store two times a year, never more, for spring and winter cleaning.

- And now?

- Two, three times a week. Some weeks more. And he dresses better.

- Has Mr. Kalich's wardrobe improved noticeably?

- Impeccable. He's a real stickler now. A regular dandy. He demands everything be perfect.

- Mrs. Markson, when did these changes regarding clothing in Mr. Kalich begin to manifest themselves?

- I can't say exactly. It happened suddenly. Overnight. Maybe a year ago.

- So, is it fair to say, Mr. Kalich wasn't like this prior to the boy and girl moving in?

- Now he bothers the life out of us. If his cuffs are an inch off, or the hem of the girl's dress half an inch, he demands we do it over again and again.

- Are Mr. Kalich's demands the same for the boy as for the girl?

- It's different. At most he might buy the boy a pair of chinos from Banana Republic, or a shirt, but the girl, only the best: Ralph Lauren, Armani, Bergdorf Goodman.

- Are there any other changes you've noticed in Mr. Kalich in this last year different from the old days?

- For years he would come into the store and not say a word to me. A frown on his face. His head buried in a book.

- And now?

- He asks me about my kids and my father. Not that my father is sick, but he is old.

- Mrs. Markson, Mr. Kalich has been a customer in your cleaning store for years, decades. How do you account for such behavioral changes?

Mrs. Markson pauses before answering.

- I always said he should have got married and had children when he had the chance. Maybe he's making up for lost time.

What the cleaning store lady said about me was true. Once the boy and girl moved in I couldn't pass a store window without seeing something I had to purchase for the girl. Especially in the first eight months, before things changed.

This afternoon I placed the television set in the boy's room, necessitating the girl to join him if she wants to watch television this evening, or any other for that matter. And, of course, there is only one seat, a loveseat, which I had most judiciously chosen when designing the room. After thirty-seven minutes of dithering, of stretches and contortions, of maneuvering her body position, closer and closer, by gradations, inches, the girl sidled over like a wounded creature and seated herself next to the boy. Before the movie ended I noticed the boy's hand, almost imperceptibly, grazing the girl's.

- Mr. Kalich, I'm more than a little surprised that you can't be more succinct on this matter.

- You forget something essential.

- And that is?

- I never really wrote the novel.

- But still, Mr. Kalich, you took such obsessive interest in the boy and girl, an obsession that has lasted for more than twenty-five years.

- I never denied that I was obsessed with the book.

- But it was more than that. It was...

- I agree. My novel "The Transfiguration of the Commonplace" was just an unending array of images and ideas that remained in my head.

- But that's just the point. Those images didn't just remain in your head. You took great pains to make them real, first in your creative vision for your novel, and then later in life...

- Do you have a question?

- Replicating to a good extent, the plot machinations of your novel.

- Do you have a question?

- Mr. Kalich, after cultivating and taking such great pains to build up the boy and girl's relationship, provide them with home and shelter, warmth and succor, as you say, why-- what possessed you, other than the compunction to follow your would-be novel's inexorable plottings, to destroy what you built?

- You've answered your own question. It's not unlike the rise and fall of the Roman Empire. History teaches us...

- Mr. Kalich, surely you can't compare your relationship with the boy and girl to the rise and fall of the Roman Empire.

- If you prefer, I'll rein in my literary allusions for the sake of clarity if nothing else.

- If you would, Mr. Kalich.

- Then think of the very common habit of probing our fingers against a rotten tooth. No doubt we're all familiar with that delectable bit of mischief.

Kalich probes his tooth.

- Or maybe it has more to do, as I also mentioned previously, with my brother's three-year-old, Knute, at play.

- But Mr. Kalich. Once you took the actual boy and girl into your home you were no longer writing a novel, and certainly not partaking in mere child's play.

- Who can say. Are you so certain when the fiction ends and true life begins? Is there such a fine dividing line in today's world?

- Mr. Kalich, metaphysical musings have little bearing in this investigation.

- On that much we agree. But still and all we are living in a world where people are extending their boundaries as to what is real or not. Everything seems possible.

- Mr. Kalich I'm more confused than ever. What do you mean when you say, or at least infer, that your book, in this case not so much your book, but notes for your book, caused the boy and girl's suicide? Or would you rather have us believe that the actual boy and girl and their suicide became the book you couldn't write?

- You don't really expect me to answer that question, do you? Indeed, that's the sole reason why we're here, to have that question answered. Certainly you have more qualified people assembled here than I to...After all, a writer can only write his book, it takes others to interpret it.

When I look back I realize the transition from creating fiction to experiencing that same fiction live-action on screen is not so much a radical change, overcoming a great divide, as opening myself to new possibilities. I was a Writer, was I not? A person who lived his life inside himself. In the imaginary realm. It was only natural for my motives to be abstract, not concrete. All I had to do was transpose my inner worlds to the outer world. Not in print but live—with a real live boy and girl at play—on screen. Rather than continue waiting for my writer's voice to muster courage and take the requisite leap of faith onto the page, I would achieve all that I had never been able to by employing a real live boy and girl to enact my obsessive fantasies. All I had to do was invite them into my lair, create the environs, choreograph the setting, set the tone and mood, plot and program the situations and scenes: Play the game. A more adventurous and enticing game I could not fathom.

Admittedly in the beginning I had only the vaguest idea where such a game would lead me. But like any game, Knute's "let's play," I was not only confident that the game would yield its due, but more importantly, that the reward was in the playing.

And, of course, once begun, I could not stop.

- Mrs. Nacheva, Mr. Kalich was the first person you befriended when you came to New York?

- My name is Katzman. Dobrinka Katzman. Nacheva was my maiden name and still is my professional name. I'm a harpist.

- And your friendship with Mr. Kalich lasted a little more than four years?

- Yes. I had just come from Bulgaria to begin studying on scholarship at Juilliard. I knew nobody in this city and Mr. Kalich took me into his life. I was only twenty and for me he was a godsend.

I have been in love two times in my life. Once, when young, with the Israeli, Hana; and twenty-eight years later, when old, with the young harpist.

- Mrs. Katzman, at the time you met Mr. Kalich, you could barely speak the language. And Mr. Kalich was a writer. What did you have to talk about?

- He wasn't really writing. At most scribbling down some notes for a future

work. And his interest in intellectual
matters, even reading books, had diminished
to a bare minimum. He mentioned that change
in himself many times over the years, as if
he could hardly believe it himself.

- I would think that must have depressed
him greatly.

- If so he didn't show it. But what did I
know. I was so young. Besides, he was in
love with me. If anything, he said I had
come into his life just in time.

- And you?

- No. I was never in love with him. But,
still, I did love him in my own way.

From the day I met Dobrinka standing in front of Juilliard,
I loved her. And if I'm honest with myself, virtually from
the beginning, once she told me her dream was to be married for fifty years like her parents and have children, I
knew she could never come to love me. Yet I persevered. If
not love, the pain was real.

- It was all in his mind. His great love
for me.

- You told Mr. Kalich that?

- Many times. In many different ways.

1. YOU WAITED TOO LONG

2. DRINKING WITH YOU WOULD BE LIKE DRINKING WITH MY MOTHER.

3. I COULD NEVER ACCEPT YOU AS A MAN.

- It must have been difficult, to say the least, for the both of you.

The harpist strums her fingers but remains mute.

- Why did you stay?

- As I said. I was young. And nobody had ever loved me like that. I remember telling him more than once: Nobody will ever love me as much as you, not even five percent.

With Hana it was all sexual. If I as much as touched her elbow she would have an orgasm. Not so with Dobrinka. Despite several flounderings we were never intimate.

- Your name is Julio Cespedes?

- Yes.

- Am I pronouncing it correctly?

- Yes.

- And you were the night doorman from the time the young harpist, Dobrinka Nacheva, moved in to reside with Mr. Kalich to the time she moved out six weeks later?

- Yes. I've been on the night shift, 12-8 a.m., for the last fifteen years in the building.

- And for that span of time, six weeks, you maintain that Mr. Kalich, at least three to four times a week, would leave his apartment to take what you call: "Night walks."

- Maybe more. I could count on it to the minute. Somewhere around 12:50 a.m. to 1:00 a.m. Mr. Kalich would exit the north elevator, race through the lobby and head out the front door. I had to hustle to keep up with him to open the door.

- Did Mr. Kalich ever say anything to you
when he raced through the lobby?

- Not a word. And I wouldn't ask. Anyone
could see he didn't want to talk.

- Can you give me an estimate, Mr.
Cespedes, as to how long Mr. Kalich's
night walks would last?

- Sometimes twenty minutes, sometimes
all night. Those times he stayed out
all night, when he returned, I hardly
recognized him. He looked terrible, as
if he had slept the night away on a park
bench.

But not so with the boy and girl. After a week, at most two,
they can't as much as walk by each other without touching:
an arm, a shoulder, a hand. Touching and pulling back and
looking guilty all at the same time.

- When my boyfriend, Alex, a French
banker, said he wasn't ready for marriage,
I had no choice but to move out.

- And you moved in with Mr. Kalich?

- I had no other place to go.

- But Mr. Kalich was in love with you.

- I was so hurt over Alex I had no room to think of anyone else...I guess I wasn't thinking.

How could she not know what her moving into my apartment would mean to me? I had waited almost three years for her to move in. Waited all my life. It was a kind of culmination for me. I had been alone all my life. Never lived with a woman. Lived half a life (as my twin deemed it). In my mind Dobrinka's moving in with me would make up for all that I had missed. Every night she would be lying there next to me in my bed, and as soon as the lights went out, she would turn her back to me and expect me to do the same. I couldn't. No matter how hard I tried I couldn't. I would feel such yearning, such longing, to touch her. Everything in me wanted to touch her, love her. It was a thousand times stronger than with Hana. It wasn't even sexual. I had waited all my life and now, finally, she moved in, and nothing...

Those six weeks were the most painful in my life.

- Mrs. Katzman, can you cite anything

specific that led you to believe Mr.
Kalich's love for you was, as you say,
in his mind?

- Not at first. But after a while, maybe
a year, several things confirmed it for
me.

- And they were?

- In his bathroom he had this great
collection of photographs in plastic
frames. Photos of his entire life,
really. And a lot of them were of
beautiful women: models, actresses,
even beauty contest winners. He would
tell me about the women. Vivienne,
Marielle, Pamela. Anyway, one day I
noticed the year 1969 written on the
back of Vivienne's photo.

- And how did your noticing the year 1969
on the back of Vivienne's photo convince
you that Mr. Kalich's love for you was all
in his mind?

- He had told me that he was occasionally
still seeing Vivienne, and that she was
young and beautiful like in the photo. But

I realized, if taken in 1969, she would already be a middle-aged woman.

- And the other thing?

- Marielle, a beautiful model, he said was still very much in his life. Not long after the Vivienne incident, I saw Marielle's photo in Elle magazine. The exact same pose as the photo in his bathroom.

- Did you confront Mr. Kalich on these occasions?

- The stories the man would make up about them. He certainly had an imagination being a writer.

The harpist smiles to herself.

- I repeat. Did you confront Mr. Kalich?

- No. What good would it have done? Let the man have his illusions with me as well as with them.

Not all the stories of the beautiful women in the photos are untrue. Hana and Dobrinka, for instance, are real. As for the rest, the dozen or so other photos: who can say? At this late date, one seems as real, or unreal, as another.

- You are the cellist, Kristina Reiko Cooper?

- Yes.

- You dated Mr. Kalich at the same time he was in love with the harpist, Dobrinka Nacheva?

- Yes. Everything he didn't say to her he said to me. He was mean. Insensitive.

- How did Mr. Kalich express this meanness?

- He was the most depressing man I ever knew. He didn't like himself enough to love anybody else.

- Ms. Cooper, you mentioned insensitivity. How was Mr. Kalich insensitive?

- Well, for example, after venting his

rage and frustrations over dinner on me,
he would then leave me in the middle of
the street to find a taxi on my own. It was
mid-winter...freezing cold.

- Did Mr. Kalich's meanness or
insensitivity ever lead to violent
behavior?

The cellist shakes her head: No.

The median time in the first month for the boy to feel suf-
ficiently comfortable to seat himself next to the girl when
watching television in the girl's room was three minutes
and thirty-seven seconds. The time increased substan-
tially, five minutes and ten seconds, if I joined them. Of
course I had purchased only one television set for both of
them. (Have I already said that?)

- Was Mr. Kalich particularly jealous of
your boyfriends, Mrs. Katzman?

- He always encouraged me to enjoy my
youth. It goes all too fast, he said.
Before you know it, it's over. He was
right.

The harpist smiles to herself.

- And so I presume you and Mr. Kalich came
to some kind of arrangement regarding your
dating activities.

- Yes and no. What he said wasn't what he
felt. Actually it wasn't just a matter
of his being jealous. He was, how do
you say it, possessive. Proprietary. He
would lecture me all the time. One time
at a concert when a young friend came to
my dressing room to talk to me, he was
furious. He shouted across the room it was
our moment of truth.

- Moment of truth?

- Yes. Either I leave with him or my young
friend. I had to choose. Or else it was
over between us. He was always threatened
by Nicholas: being young, handsome, an
actor. I think it was Nicholas' being
an actor that particularly bothered him.
In any case, he was always giving me
ultimatums like that.

- And whom did you leave with?

- Nicholas, of course.

- And Mr. Kalich?

- He followed us and a little later,
after I left Nicholas to go upstairs to my
apartment, he confronted him on Columbus
Avenue while he was waiting for a taxi.

- You are Nicholas Bellinger?

- Yes.

- You are Ms. Nacheva's friend, the actor.

- Yes.

- You escorted Ms. Nacheva home from the
concert that night when Mr. Kalich stalked
you and eventually confronted you after
Ms. Nacheva returned to her apartment?

- Yes.

- Please cite, Mr. Bellinger, what
transpired between you and Mr. Kalich that
night after Ms. Nacheva returned to her
apartment.

- Sure. Look, I admit to taunting him a
little. I mean when we were standing up
the block, in front of Dobri's building,
and I looked back and saw him following
us, stalking us, I raised my arm as if
waving to him. But after Dobri went up to
her apartment, when I was on the corner
waiting for a cab, the old guy came up to
me. He was crazed. I told him I wasn't
going to walk away, but after one look
I could see it was him who wasn't going
to walk away. This was no scene from one
of my acting classes; this was real. He
was capable of anything at that moment, I
thought. Love will do that to you I guess.
Anyway, when a cab pulled up I jumped in
and took off.

What agonies and humiliations I endured for years over
Dobrinka. And now when I look back I ask myself: why?
why? Fortunately I've learned my lesson. I won't repeat my
mistakes with the boy and girl.

- One last question, Mrs. Katzman.

- Yes.

- How did Mr. Kalich respond when you

finally married Mr. Katzman? A very
successful businessman, our records
indicate, I might add.

- He didn't respond. Or rather I should
say he never came to the wedding despite
my sending him an invitation. And leaving
two very personal invites on his answering
machine. And it was a lovely affair, five
hundred guests, at the Rainbow Room. We
haven't talked since.

One can learn much from the old people in the building. The way Carmilly dresses every day in his suit and
tie, hat on head, hunchbacked and frail, he'll be ninety-six
next month, takes his daily walk. The old man never flags,
never misses a paddle-like step. One month after returning
from the hospital for a fractured hip he was at it again. His
only concession: a walker. And Max Klozzner, the award-
winning photographer. Ninety-one if a day. The way he
suddenly stops in the middle of the street, people and traf-
fic scurrying by, to concentrate his gaze on a child, any
child, passing in the flow. His entire being seems to come
to concentrated attention as he gazes upon the child, a
half grin or inward smile on his face, eyes glinting, almost
ready to burst into laughter, it's as if he's contemplating a
great work of art in a museum. One gets the feeling that

Max sees what others do not. And, yes, the old people never fail to greet each other. They can talk, laugh, smile and converse for hours while others jolt by with a cab to catch, a meeting to make, and a taut, tense expression on their faces. I'm certain that Carmilly gets as much from his walk around the block, his half block stroll in the park, and Max from his gaze, as the others do from all their combined trips to China, Aspen and/or Dubai.

Can I gain as much from observing my boy and girl on screen?

> - Would you like to add to or explain that last statement by the harpist, Mr. Kalich?
>
> - Which one was that?
>
> - That you haven't talked since.

Observing the boy and girl on screen, spending time with them inside the apartment or out, is no longer essential for my purposes. In recent weeks, whether alone by myself or in the midst of a crowd, their images never leave me. My mind is constantly churning with ideas for our next encounter.

- You are Robert Kalich?

- Yes.

- You are the twin brother of Richard Kalich?

- Yes.

- You are, like your brother, a writer?

- A writer, yes. But a very different kind of writer.

- How does your writing differ from your brother Richard's?

- That's not easy to explain. First off, Dick's a literary fiction writer. I'm more commercial.

- And secondly?

- Like all twins, I would think, we're opposite sides of the same coin. In our case that translates to my being a body writer, visceral, spontaneous. I love writing. He, on the other hand, is cerebral, mental; craft and cunning are his strengths. He hates writing.

- Cunning?

- Craft then. Once he sees his novel, has his metaphor, he has the beginning, middle and end. I have to write a thousand pages to get my three hundred. Put us together and you'd have one hell of a novelist.

- Are there any other differences, not so much in style or technique, but...

- For Dick everything has to be perfect. He has to wrench every word out of himself. Every word is torture.

- But you just said your brother sees his novel whole. And once he does, he has his beginning, middle and...

- I know, but I also said he hates writing. He's convoluted. Look, writing or otherwise, Dick can't escape who he is. And for him writing was everything. It was his raison d'être. Ever since we were in our teens and read the great Russians, he had to be Dostoevski or nothing.

- And you?

- It wasn't as important. I mean I wrote
the best novel I could, but it was never
a matter of life and death. I had other
things in my life.

- Other things?

- A wife, two actually, and children. A boy
and a girl. One from each marriage. I always
had intimacy, the love of a woman, the love
of children. Dick never did. With twins what
one does the other doesn't need to.

- So for Richard writing was too
important?

- For Dick everything is too important.

In my late teens I loved baseball. I played high school baseball and organized ball. One day I got hit on the elbow
by a pitch and, after standing on second base for a few
minutes in great pain, I trotted off the field. I never played
baseball again. Other kids said it was because of my fear
of being hit by the ball, but it wasn't that. I just realized I
wasn't going to be the next Mickey Mantle.

- I would think, Mr. Kalich, that you
being Richard's twin, you would know him
better than anyone else in the world.

- What's your point?

- I know this is difficult for you, Mr.
Kalich.

- Is there a question?

- Do you think your twin capable of
causing injury or harm to the boy and
girl?

- No, definitely not, but then again I
really don't know him as well as you might
think.

- You don't know him?!

There is no such thing as knowing oneself much less another human being. No time was this more apparent in
my life than when I finished writing my first novel, "The
Nihilesthete." I didn't have the slightest idea what I had. A
madman's ravings or a novel. It was a veritable Rorschach
test which I had to give to others to interpret.

- Can you explain what you mean when you say you don't know your brother as well as you might think?

- For example, when he finished his novel, "The Nihilesthete." He hadn't mentioned a word about it to me all through the writing, and then when he finally gave it to me to read: I couldn't believe it. It was a complete shock. I had no idea he had that in him.

- And what was it that your brother, Richard, had in him?

- All that sadism, perversity, grotesqueness. I mean the novel was brilliant, but as for the rest...I was totally unprepared.

- Do you think, and again I know this is difficult for you, Mr. Kalich, but do you think he could somehow transfer such venom and brutality from the written page to real people? Namely the boy and girl?

- Look, it was fiction. "The Nihilesthete" was a brilliant metaphoric work of fiction. As for the relationship he had with the

boy and girl, I couldn't begin to make
heads or tails of it. Your guess is as
good as mine. Ricki, my first wife, always
said: Dick will do something and then come
up with a philosophy to justify it.

- You haven't answered my question, Mr.
Kalich.

- I think I have.

There's a method to my madness. Whether I take a stroll
through the park or a seat at the corner Starbucks, the trick
is to sharpen my hunter's eye. That achieved, plotting and
programming ideas for the boy and girl unfold as abun-
dantly as the flora and fauna in a tropical forest. All that
remains is to allow the images and ideas to filter through
my brain, jot down notes until my pack of 3x5 cards is as
thick and choice-laden as Time Warner Cable's programming selection; and then pick and choose one scenario
or another, whatever turbulence and mayhem, reward or
punishment, catches my fancy to play for the night.

- Can you tell us anything else about your
brother that would help us to understand
how he could even come to write such a
novel; a novel, I should indicate, that

has been described as one of the darkest
in American fiction? And more importantly,
I apologize, but I must ask again: can
you tell us why he would invite this
particular boy and girl into his home and
possibly cause them harm and injury?

- I already told you. I can't. But I can
tell you he was always strange. Weird.
Different.

- In what way was your twin brother
Richard different?

- He lived half a life. No sex. No
intimacy. Right out of Winesburg, Ohio. I
told him that all the time.

- What do you mean: your brother lived
"half a life"?

- He was never integrated. Never able
to find a balance. For him, life was
books, ideas, writing, the interior
life. Everything else he categorically
dismissed. Married life, family, home,
creature comforts meant little or nothing
to him. For example, he lived seven years
in PH-F before he even bought a TV or air

conditioner. He was always alone. He never
lived with a woman. And when Knute was
small, despite living only six or seven
blocks from us, he never visited. Never
once came over to play with him. Take him
to a movie or to the circus. Even to the
park. He would chronically say: "What's he
got to do with my life?!" Imagine, his own
nephew. So self-absorbed. I had to beg him
to babysit and even then...

- And yet he fell deeply in love with the
young harpist, Ms. Nacheva.

- I wouldn't call that love.

- What would you call it?

- A pathetic and desperate attempt to make
up for the life he never lived. Besides,
he has bigger problems than the harpist.

After the boy and girl's first embrace I celebrated the
occasion by suggesting that the boy would have to begin paying an increased rent for his lodgings; knowing
full well, of course, that he had no means to do so. The
squint-eyed glances and conspiratorial whispers shared a
few minutes later between the two in a favorite hiding

place was all the return I needed. After careful consideration I soon told them that the increased rent would not be necessary. We all have to make sacrifices, including myself, I said. Once again there was joy in PH-F.

- You've mentioned more than once, Mr. Kalich, that your twin was always angry, sad, depressed. That everything bothered him. And that the young harpist was only the smallest part of the problem. A symptom, not a cause, as you put it. Could you elaborate further to help us understand his problem? Perhaps give us a rationale?

- You mean besides the complete present day collapse of the literary culture? That though acknowledged by some of the best literary minds in the world for having written two first rate novels, his advances and royalty payments were a joke? He used to say for every "yes" he received in his life, he received a thousand "no's."

"The Nihilesthete" was rejected by seventy-five publishers before a small independent press in Sag Harbor committed to publish it. It cost me five years of almost single-minded pathological pursuit to find that publisher. My second novel, "Charlie P," went somewhat easier. Only thirty-five rejection letters. During those five years pursuing a publisher for "The Nihilesthete," I was so depressed I literally couldn't lift my pen to write a single line.

- By your words, Mr. Kalich, am I to infer that it's even more difficult for writers such as your brother today?

- Definitely. At least when we were young, starting out, there was the possibility of being published. Of making a name for yourself. Today nothing. The entire literary culture is dead. It's been appropriated by the pop culture. Writers such as my brother have been rendered obsolete, irrelevant, superfluous, no different than disposable goods. Whatever adjective you want to use. From redeeming the world with the word it's come down to iPods and video games, TV and computers, Kindles and Nooks. His meta-fictions and philosophical novels, like "Transfiguration of the Commonplace," have turned into Donald Trump's reality TV. Dick always said he wanted to write a novel about it someday.

Literature Ruined My Life: I promised myself that one day I would write a novel with that as its title.

- Mr. Kalich. This is neither the time nor place to hold court or make use of the podium for a diatribe against the plight of the literary culture.

- I'm sorry but...

- Obviously you feel strongly on the subject.

- The subject is my twin brother.

- Right. Quite right. But for that reason, if no other, I must ask you to stay all the closer to the subject at hand. This is an interrogation, after all. You are under obligation...

- Do you have a question?

- Was there anything in your brother's life, and I mean to say his actual life, not so much his writing life, that would lead him to perpetrate some kind of violence...

101

- Didn't you just stop me from answering
that same question?

- That would, because of his various
depressive moods, possibly lead him into
arguments when angry, or even, perhaps,
physical confrontations?

The twin remains silent.

- Mr. Kalich, even if this is not a
conventional court of law, it is an
interrogation. I must remind you that you
are under obligation to answer...

- Answer what?

One starts out one's life reading the great writers.
Dostoevski, Hesse, Mann, Camus, West, Kafka. You ex-
alt their pain and suffering, deprivation and denials, to
the level of martyrdom; apotheosize and canonize their
artistry to the realm of the absolute. And then one day at
the age of fifty, or sixty, it dawns on you that not only do
your own books belong on the same shelf as theirs, but
your own tattered writer's life has not been that different
from their own.

- You say there was one time, Mr. Kalich?

- Yes. About fifteen to twenty years ago.
We were both working for the Department
of Social Services and I remember my twin
and I being called into the Director's
office for some nonsense or not. I think
it was, yes, it was field time and how we
both abused it. Anyway, the Director was
a harmless bureaucrat and when he started
lecturing my brother about field time
and how staff was expected to make each
and every visit and such...my brother
just exploded. Verbally decimated the
Director. By the time my brother was
finished there was nothing left of the
man. It seemed to me that my brother
vented a lifetime's frustration and anger
in that one tirade.

MEMORANDUM

I.610(77)

January 17, 1983

Ms Carolyn Shipp, Supvr. Team B
GSS/M-11

re: Richard Kalich

Mr. Bill Murphy, Director
GSS/M-11

Audit Field-Time

A Timekeeping Audit was conducted during the months
of November and December of all GSS Field staff
(500 casemanagers).

The findings indicate that District M-11 is basically
in compliance with procedure, but we were instructed
to follow-up on two worker's field-time.

Please forward to my office by the C.O.B. on Jan. 21,
1983 a written statement from you (Supvr.) and
casemanager answers for the following questions.

(1) Why worker has continually checked out for
field each working day for three (3) years.
(Audit state that worker has only spent 15
days in office in a spand of three years).

(2) Does worker have a special case load which
would be necessary for him to check out to
field each p.m.?

(3) Have his field time been approved by Supvr.
(Team Supvr.)?

(4) How many clients does worker visit during
his visits to field?

(5) Is it necessary for worker to check out for
field each day in p.m.?

When I worked for the Department I sat next to a woman (I've forgotten her name) who would say in emotive, heartfelt tones, daily, after a telephone call with a client, an interview, or returning to the office from a field visit: "I love my clients!" And then would turn to face me. I, in turn, could do no more than shake my head and smile.

- And that was it? It went no further?

- No. But until that time I never really understood how much it cost my brother to live the life he did.

- And by living the life he did you mean to say: Half a life?

The twin sighs and manages a barely perceptible nod.

- Final question, Mr. Kalich. Would all these difficulties your brother experienced: loss of authority, having little or no place in the community, being rendered obsolete, irrelevant, superfluous, would all these difficulties combined be sufficient cause to catalyze a kind of monstrous egotism in your...

- I don't understand the question.

- Let me put it another way. Would all
your brother's hardship and travail be
reason enough for him to assume more
extreme behavior than mere manifestations
of anger, bitterness, melancholy,
including the possibility of his
perpetrating violence, harm and injury on
the boy and girl?

The twin ponders the question.

- You really must answer the question, Mr.
Kalich.

- I'll say this only once. To the best of
my knowledge my twin brother was never
happier, more content and at peace with
himself than when he took in the boy and
girl to live with him in PH-F.

	RICHARD (DICK) "SUNRISE"	ROBERT (BOB) "SUNSET"
1. EARLY CHILDHOOD	(Mother's appellation for happy, smiling child.)	(Mother's appellation for chronically moody and unhappy child.)
2. EARLY MEMORY	Readily eats mother's spoon-fed meals and feels sorry for mother when twin doesn't do so.	Holds spoonfuls in mouth to point where his swollen cheeks look like Popeye the sailor. Twin, Dick, empathizes with mother's pain and frustration and encourages brother to swallow.

	RICHARD (DICK)	ROBERT (BOB)
3. SPORTS CHILDHOOD	First chosen by friends for city games (curb ball, punchball, stickball, baseball) and stars at shortstop and centerfield.	Chronically chosen last, if at all, to play city games with peers and friends; and then to play right field and catcher. Often frustrated by lack of athletic aptitude and often storms off home in tears and anger.
4. BAR MITZVAH	Assumes total responsibility; loses 20 pounds due to stress as it's a major event in household as father is renowned cantor in orthodox European synagogue.	Rebels against orthodox father– the cantor–and Jewish protocol and expectancies and lets brother make up for his laxity.

	RICHARD (DICK)	ROBERT (BOB)
5. Post Bar Mitzvah	Day after bar mitzvah, staring teary-eyed into father's bedroom mirror, cuts tephillin with scissors from arm and vows never to speak to father again or go to synagogue.	Continues to go his own way, in flagrant disregard of parents' wishes and expectancies of "good Jewish son."
6. College	Attends academically demanding City College of New York. Takes schoolwork all too seriously. All study and no play makes for bookish and stressful college years.	Attends NYU. Never studies. Four years of fun and games.

	RICHARD (DICK)	ROBERT (BOB)
7. MILITARY SERVICE	Six (6) months army reserves and five-and-one-half years of obligation. Latrine Orderly every summer.	Feigns neurological defect of hands to avoid U.S. Army service.
8. LOVE	Except for six (6) week period with the young harpist, never lives with a woman. Loves only two women in his lifetime, once when young, another when old; both times "breaking down" when romance didn't work out.	Two wives, children, boy and girl, one from each marriage. Shares intimacy and love throughout his life. Also has three live-in girlfriends for five years each; and more than his share of sexual liaisons.

	RICHARD (DICK)	ROBERT (BOB)
9. ADULT YEARS	Lives "half a life" (brother's coinage). Books and writing, little else. Saves nickels and dimes. Never leaves Manhattan and becomes, in later years, increasingly isolated and reclusive.	Handicapper, gambler, man-about-town. Gregarious, social; lives life to the fullest, most often at other people's (especially twin's) expense.
10. WORK	Hates job as case worker for Dept. of Social Services, finding it humiliating and debasing.	Professional handicapper and gambler.

	RICHARD (DICK)	ROBERT (BOB)
11. WRITING	Hates writing, suffering from creative block. Constantly judging himself. Dostoevski or nothing–and for this reason constipated, self-conscious, and terrified of "letting go."	Loves writing. Visceral, spontaneous. Body writer. Lets it all hang out knowing he has a built-in genetic fail safe in his twin who in effect functions as his "Maxwell Perkins."
12. CHARACTER	Serious to a fault, makes everything too important from writing to shopping for a new suit. Nothing easy or relaxed.	Excessive. Large appetites, large dreams. Lives fast and easy knowing if he can't pay his bills, his bookmakers, credit cards and financial debts, he

	RICHARD (DICK)	ROBERT (BOB)
12. CHARACTER (CONTINUED)		always has his twin to do it for him. Invents persona, "Broadway Bob," and not only sells it to the world but believes it himself. Rich and successful.
13 MONEY	Scrimps and saves; every dollar accounted for. Never borrows, not a cent, neither from friends nor credit card companies. Scrupulously honest.	Gambles excessively. Lives big and spends bigger to keep up appearances. Picks up every bill. If he can't pay bills, like with writing, he always has his twin to bail him out.

	RICHARD (DICK)	ROBERT (BOB)
14. Travel and Vacations	Never travels. Never vacations. Rarely, if ever, leaves Manhattan. Maybe one half-vacation in last 28 years and that to a book fair to help promote his own book.	Constant traveling and vacationing, usually at other people's expense.

```
- If anything, Mr. Kalich, this chart
shows you cannot attribute the differences
between your brother and yourself, as well
as your unhappiness and dissatisfaction
with your life, to your difficulties and
struggles as a writer; nor your being
victimized by the diachronic illusion
centering around the transvaluation of the
literary culture to the electronic culture.
You must assume some responsibility too.
```

I remain unresponsive, once again not giving the interrogator the satisfaction of an answer.

```
- Even you, Mr. Kalich, must admit that much.

- Mr. Kalich, what do you mean you are no
longer that person anymore?

- Something inside me has changed.

- But, Mr. Kalich, all your life you've
loved books. You've savored their words,
contemplated their meanings, reflected over
them, surrendered yourself to them, immersed
yourself in them. Don't you feel you've lost
something essential as to who you are?

- Whatever.
```

I escorted the girl to dinner tonight at an elegant Eastside restaurant. It was the first time in at least a month that we were able to be completely alone. To make our way to the dining area we had to pass through a crowded bar section. Wholly unexpectedly, the girl took my hand to help me cross the low threshold into the restaurant. For those brief moments her warm hand laid in mine I felt ecstasy. In my mind I couldn't have been closer to her. I can't remember the last time a woman either took my hand or I experienced such warm, intimate feelings. It confirmed for me what I had already come to sense watching the girl on screen with the boy. How her intimate glances and gestures observed by me on screen are meant as much for me as the boy. After dinner, which was more than pleasant, I don't think I stopped talking once other than to gulp down several particularly large mouthfuls of filet mignon; and, of course, the food was excellent, not that I'm a gourmet; on the contrary, I hardly know how or what to order from an Italian menu, but I did enjoy the elegant atmosphere. At any rate, I was in the midst of telling the girl that I had a real treat in store for her. There was an ice cream parlor in the immediate area famous for its pastries and desserts; the girl, to be sure, has a sweet tooth, loves chocolate ice cream and virtually any kind of cake. So imagine my surprise and disappointment when, even before I could finish my sentence, the girl was already telling me she would rather return home. Her stomach felt queasy. I immediately signaled for a taxi. But once home, after first making certain I had entered my room, the way the girl surreptitiously headed directly to the boy's room, I understood instantly that her desire to return home had little to do with any kind of stomach ailment, but rather that she wished to satisfy another kind of appetite. One no ice cream parlor catered to other than in sublimated portions.

Needless to say, I stayed up late that night wracking my brain over ways to satisfy my own appetites.

- You are Mr. Charles Leiser?

- Charlie Leiser. Call me Charlie.
Everybody else does.

- You are the proprietor of a bookstand on 68th Street and Columbus Avenue where you sell old, used and out-of-print books?

- I don't know much about being a proprietor, but I do have a bookstand on West 68th Street.

- And for the past twenty years or more, Mr. Kalich has been a customer?

- For years he couldn't pass my stand without stopping to browse for at least thirty to forty minutes. Some days we'd spend the whole afternoon talking about books and writers.

- And in addition to literary talk, I assume Mr. Kalich also purchased your books.

- If I had ten customers like Kalich in those days, I'd be retired by now.

- What do you mean by "in those days"?

- I mean that was another time, another Kalich.

- Another Mr. Kalich. Please explain.

- There was a period for about eight to ten years that he stopped coming around. Didn't as much as wave his hand when passing, much less stop to buy a book.

- And this stoppage happened prior to the boy and girl taking up residence in Mr. Kalich's apartment?

- It happened years before they showed up. But I have to admit once the young people moved in with him, he started coming round again. Even if it wasn't to buy books.

- If Mr. Kalich no longer purchased books, what did he purchase from your bookstand?

- Illustrated books from the '20s and '30s; Ziegfeld Follies memorabilia; and fashion and photography magazines with famous models and actresses on their covers. The last item I remember him buying was an old Life magazine with Marilyn Monroe on its cover.

- Did Mr. Kalich frequent your bookstand with the boy and girl?

- Are you kidding? Who do you think be bought that stuff for? That little girl pulled him around by the nose.

- Please explain the phrase: pulled him around by the nose.

- As I said, the girl had him buy fashion magazines and illustrated books for her, but the real reason they came round is because my stand is located just one block from a women's shop up the block. She was always dragging him there to shop for a dress for her or something. Actually, it was him probably dragging her. Wherever he went, he was always window-shopping for her.

- Mr. Leiser, earlier you made mention of another turnaround in Mr. Kalich that occurred just several months prior to the boy and girl's suicide.

- That's right. It was like that ten-year stoppage period all over again. For some reason he lost interest in shopping for the girl the same way he lost interest years back with books.

- All shopping?

- In those months I never once saw him go into the women's shop with or without the girl.

At a certain point in writing, a Writer becomes his character and from that time on, as already mentioned, does little more than take dictation. In a similar manner, an

Actor, after having read, practiced, rehearsed his/her role for a week, a month or more, becomes the character he/she is to play. It's not so much that the two become one as the Writer/Actor becoming the other. Though, of course, both still retain that which is most significant about themselves and bring that unique material to the task at hand. Like a Writer, like an Actor, I have become one with the boy and girl. When I observe them now on screen, there is hardly a difference between what I see and who I am. All the girl's smiles, gestures, touches, caresses, lovemaking with the boy, I feel are meant as much for me as for him. I am indeed a fortunate man. Like in all good writing, in all creation, a miracle has been wrought. What has for so long laid dormant deep inside me, the boy and girl have mined and feelings and emotions I no longer knew I even possessed have been unleashed like buried treasure to become part and parcel of my everyday. For the first time in years I feel truly alive.

    - Mr. Martinez, you are the Director
    of the Guadalupe Halfway House in East
    Harlem?

    - I am.

What will I in turn bring to the boy and girl?

- And it was your decision to place the boy and girl into Mr. Kalich's home.

- Yes.

- Mr. Martinez, it's been established that Mr. Kalich had, by his own admission, a great antipathy for practicing social work, abused his field time privileges when he was employed, found the bureaucratic system demeaning as well as spiritually deadening, and even possessed such disdain and loathing for his fellow civil service peers that he confronted them verbally if not physically more than once over the years.

- Yes. I'm aware of that.

- And yet still you maintain that Mr. Kalich is a great social worker? A caring and compassionate man?

- Most definitely.

- What in your experience has led you to such a conclusion?

- Because I know Mr. Kalich, not only as a professional colleague, but also as a client.

- A client?

- Yes.

- Please explain.

- As you can see I'm a quadriplegic. At eleven years of age I was a member of the Cuban National Olympic Swimming Team when it was my poor fate to dive into a pool of concrete, causing a severe spinal cord injury and my resulting quadriplegic condition. Two years later my father, brother and I settled in New York City. My father took a job as a janitor for Columbia University, and my brother, Celso, always a difficult spirit, soon enough found himself interred at Rikers Island. Mr. Kalich was assigned to my case as caseworker. Thanks to his social work efforts I am where I am today.

- Can you be more specific? Perhaps give an example or...

- I have your assurances that these proceedings are private?

- You do. The outside world has no interest in what transpires here.

- All right then. Mr. Kalich arranged
home care service for me and though
I only required a home attendant for
four hours a day, twenty-eight hours a
week, Mr. Kalich provided home attendant
service for twelve hours per day, eighty-
four hours a week. Those extra hours the
home attendant didn't have to work added
up to quite a tidy sum in additional
salary earnings which were divided
equally between myself and the home
attendant. It goes without saying that
that money afforded me the opportunity to
make the most of my difficult situation.
And that, along with Mr. Kalich's
constant encouragement, motivated me not
only to finish high school, but go on
to college and even acquire a Masters
degree in Social Work at Long Island
University, and ultimately assume the
position I presently hold as Director of
the Guadalupe Halfway House.

I might also add that Antonio Martinez recently married,
finding a mail order bride from his native Cuba, and with
the aid of a dangerous (for him) penile implant operation,
functions quite satisfactorily with his young wife.

- Your name is Knute?

- Yes.

- You know Mr. Richard Kalich?

- Of course. He's my father's twin brother.

- And that makes him your uncle.

- Yes. Uncle Dickie. He's my second favorite uncle.

- Who is your first favorite uncle?

- Uncle Johnny. He takes me everywhere when he comes to New York from California. He's my favorite uncle.

- But it was your uncle Dick who took you to see the Lion King play, was it not?

- That was only because Mommy was sick and Bobby was out of town on business.

The boy lowers his eyes to avert his uncle's gaze.

- Before the Lion King play started, Knute, didn't your uncle also take you to another theater to purchase tickets for another play?

- Yes. He said he could kill two birds with one stone.

- And what was that second play?

- Romeo and Juliet. He wanted the tickets for the boy and girl living with him.

- And what did you say to that?

- I don't remember.

- Didn't you mention something about other plays?

- Oh yeah. I told him they would probably have more fun seeing other plays.

- What other plays?

- I don't know. Tarzan, Lion King, or maybe movies like Cars, Shrek III, even The Fantastic Mr. Fox.

- Did your uncle say why, of all the plays and movies available, he chose Romeo and Juliet for the boy and girl to see?

The boy doesn't answer.

- Your uncle said nothing?

- Maybe it was because he wanted the boy and girl to love each other like Romeo and Juliet love each other.

- Your uncle said that?

- No.

- Who then?

- Me.

- And what did your uncle say when you said that?

- He didn't say anything. But he smiled.

- And how do you remember that he smiled?

- Because Uncle Dickie never smiles.

The boy lowers his eyes.

    - This next question is very important,
    Knute.

    - I thought all the questions are
    important.

    - Yes. But this is the most important one.
    Did your Uncle Dick mention what happens to
    Romeo and Juliet at the end of the play?

The boy remains silent.

    - He didn't say anything?

The boy shakes his head. Lowers his eyes, but almost immediately looks up.

    - Tell me. What happens to Romeo and
    Juliet at the end of the play?

When the idea for double suicide first took root, who but I could have traced its origins back to my unfortunate experience with Dobrinka at the women's store where she chose her white dress from the Romeo and Juliet catalogue?

Strange how the mind works. Stranger still how things ultimately fall into place. I wonder if all people are like me. Not merely storytellers, but storymakers at heart, having the wherewithal to make chaos into harmony.

- At the women's store where Ms. Nacheva selected the dress from the Romeo and Juliet catalogue, you had no idea at the time that it would play such an integral role in the boy and girl's double suicide?

- How could I? I didn't even know the boy and girl at the time.

- And later when you did get to know the boy and girl?

- Later, for the first time in my life, I was at peace with myself and completely happy with the boy and girl.

- You were happy and at peace with yourself?

- As I and others have said: For the longest time.

The Interrogator even has the temerity to question me about a childhood incident that I would have much preferred to forget.

- So, Mr. Kalich, this recurring theme
of suicide, according to your previous
testimony, I have to assume might have
originated in a childhood incident when
you were seven or eight years old and you
witnessed the suicide of a childhood friend
on 104th Street and West End Avenue.

- Yes. I can still see my friend's
shattered body lying in an ever-widening
pool of blood.

- And that image of your little friend and
the ever-widening pool of blood you've
remembered all these years?

- That along with his grief-stricken
mother's words to his father.

- And what were those words?

- You drove him to it. You drove him to
it. She repeated those words over and over
again.

Not too long ago the girl would listen with
to my every word, now I notice she waits i
me to finish, and then, instantly, either offe
ing stare, or skulks away to join the boy.

- And when things changed?

- When the boy and girl changed suddenly,
as if overnight, all sorts of ideas,
thoughts, feelings came over me.

- What kinds of ideas?

- Naturally I had to make adjustments.

- What kinds of adjustments?

Then there are times when a deeper, more primal voice
breaks through. A voice that does not mince words, but
speaks only of essentials. An unrestrained voice, untram-
meled by conventions, that no court of law's protocols can
restrict or restrain.

- And such a voice came to you that night
in the elevator with the young harpist?

- I realized for the first time I would

never be with Dobrinka. I would always be
alone, for the rest of my life, alone.

- And that was the first time you
realized...?

- I had nothing to fight for her with.

- What do you mean you had nothing to fight
for her with?

- I was already old, sexually impotent, a
sense of profound powerlessness pervaded
my entire being.

- And yet you surrendered yourself
completely to the young harpist. Gave all
you had to give.

- On some level I must have known that all
I had given to Dobrinka was nothing more
than compensation for the life I never
lived.

- And so, already old, without love or
books, by way of recompense you chose
another path?

- It was my chance to turn dross into gold.

- Your erstwhile novel. The boy and girl.
You brought them to life.

- When I saw them on screen they became
real.

- Or less real as the case may be.

- Manageable.

- You saw them as a game to be played. Toy
marionettes. Your creation.

- A man can only take so much.

- And by your own admission, the girl was
as much yours as the boy's.

All this talk, all these people, with their different vantage
points, their different interpretations. All of them know
me, or claim they do, and yet all of them know nothing
of what is true and real. All my long years of struggle and
sacrifice, all my years of aloneness, powerlessness and impotence, all those years of being less than I wanted, less
than I needed to be.

```
        - And then one night in the elevator with
        Dobrinka, the voice, my voice, "I" cried
        out: Who's going to love me?! Who's going
        to love me?!
```

Once the voice dies down, that evening or the next, I am in
my TV room again, observing the boy and girl on screen.

BIRTHDAY PRESENTS:

1. CASHMERE BLANKET.................................$440.00

2. PIN...$30.00

3. SHOES..$55.00

4. CHANEL..$106.00

5. Dress (Henry Bendel)...............................$340.00

6. Skirt (Henry Bendel)................................$145.00

7. TEDDY BEAR..$14.00

8. CHOCOLATE BIRTHDAY CAKE...................$50.00

9. Indochine's Restaurant............................$120.00

10. Taxi fare..$18.00

11. Miscellaneous...$15.00

TOTAL EXPENSES.......................................$1333.00

- You spent more than a week preparing for the girl's birthday present?

- It was a special occasion.

- You purchased many different presents for the girl?

- Each and every gift I selected I knew she would personally value.

- Including a teddy bear?

- Since a child she had always slept with a teddy. And the one she had brought with her from the halfway house was worn and raggedy.

- And you special-ordered a queen-size cashmere blanket from the Polo Baby Shop?

- I got the idea from years back when I had purchased a cashmere blanket for my twin's newborn.

- And then you dined at Indochine's?

- Yes.

- A very fashionable restaurant. And
indeed costly, especially for a person
living on social security and a small
pension.

- I had calculated what I could spend, and all
things considered, it was within my means.

- Afterwards, you returned home?

- Yes.

- It would be only natural for you to want
to share the moment. Have a nightcap with
the girl, perhaps.

- That would have been nice.

- After all, it was a special occasion, as
you say.

- The girl's 18th birthday.

- And then what happened?

- The girl said she was tired, exhausted
really, and retired to bed.

- And the boy?

- He had had as much to eat and drink as she, and was likewise eager for bed.

- Leaving you alone.

- Not really alone. I too retired, only not to bed.

- But rather to your TV room to observe the boy and girl making passionate love.

There was a moment when the girl peered directly into the camera with a complicit smile on her face. That smile proved to me that my vague suspicions were real, that this moment did truly exist. If truly meant for the boy, why then would she so glaringly aim her smile so directly into the camera? That complicit smile reconfirmed for me all that I had conjured and hoped for. The girl's smile had a basis in reality. It was as much meant for me as the boy. I was not deluding myself. I was not confusing fiction and fact. This was no fantasy on my part. The girl's complicit smile was real and the girl's love for me was real: Not merely in my head.

- When you observed the boy and girl making passionate love, you were crushed.

- No.

- Devastated.

- Not at all.

- After all, if not for you they wouldn't have clean sheets, much less a cashmere blanket; not to mention sundry other gifts as well as Chanel in the girl's room.

In the beginning the girl shared all her secrets with me. Her most intimate memories: Her preference for oral sex. Her sole experience of coitus with a man, in a vacated elementary school on a staircase.

- And so you decided to enact your cruel fantasies on the boy and girl as a way of...

- On the contrary, those intimacies expressed by the boy and girl had quite an opposite effect on me.

- Opposite?!

- Romantic obsession, pathological

jealousy, I had left that all behind me with the young harpist. I had no wish to revisit my past Molière comedy with the boy and girl.

- Then what?

- My intentions were on a higher plane.

- Please explain what you mean by higher plane?

- As I've stated all along, my primary motive was play.

- Play?!

- Yes. The very fact that the boy and girl took their lovemaking so seriously as to hide it from me only made me realize all the more that I was on the right path. After all, what did they know other than their own childish libidinal needs for each other. While I...I was the one observing them and not the other way around.

- But, by your own admission, you were on the outside looking in?

- Not outside but someplace else. In between, if you will. The boy and girl allowed me to recapture my old author's authority.

"Literature is fundamentally ludic in nature. Formidable advantages that ludic systems offer, precisely as laboratories of recherché, they allow people (authors) to test ideas in a circumscribed field of inquiry. According to a set of protocols, in a manner that is both useful and amusing."
—Johan Huizinga

"The function of a poet still remains fixed in the play-sphere where it was born. Poieses in fact, is play function. It proceeds within the playground of the mind, in a world of its own which the mind creates for it. There things have a different physiognomy from the ones they wear in ordinary life, and are bound by ties other than those of logic and causality."
— Johan Huizinga

- So fiction had truly become life for you, Mr. Kalich.

- On the contrary, life had become fiction.

I was once again a Writer taking dictation
from my characters. It only follows that
I was interested in experimenting with
my characters. Testing their limits.
Exploring just who the boy and girl were
if only for the sake of the novel I could
not write.

- And you achieved this by exacting callous
punishments on the boy and girl as if they
were mere mannequins, puppets, icons on a
game board to be manipulated at your whim.

- You miss the point entirely. If enacting
callous punishments came into play, it had
more to do with method, a mere by-product of
my intent rather than any particular goal.
For certain, I held no personal animosity
toward the boy and girl.

But who can say what's inside a man. One has to write the
book to truly know what's in it.

And even then...

Sometimes I take a break from observing the boy and girl
on screen in the TV room and reread my notes from my
original but aborted novel: "The Transfiguration of the

Commonplace." Rough and unedited as they are, it is always interesting to look back and compare these notes with my current situation. Not only do they furnish me with ideas as to how to proceed with the boy and girl, but they additionally show me what my writer's imagination was like years back when I started. How my original vision for the novel has changed, grown, progressed, and yet how closely the two still parallel and feed off each other. I defy any person, whether literary critic, scholar or common reader, to separate and differentiate between the two. For me at least, the two have become one.

* See Notes for "Transfiguration of the Commonplace."

```
                        Dis  ——→  Mow? competent
   METABHYSICIAN  OUT  TO  CAPTURE
   Transcendence  WITH  A  CAMERA."
   tran    || NOTES ||  ⊕
              TRANSFIGURATION OF THE COMMONPLACE

     Robert Habemran, an old retired social worker, looks to
restore his life, add meaning and purpose to his burned out,
used up, meaningless futiele wasted esxistence. He has an
idea. He builds a tv studio in his cloistered closet. Finds
and takes in a boy and girl, the quintessence of youth
to observe on his screen, to peek in and get a birds
view of all that he missed, wasted, didn't partake in
afn and take advantaege of. As the boy and girl cmmence
their relationship Haberman becomes involved. He too
falls in love, becomes enamored, finds youth and meaning,
his life is once  again funf and for the first time in the
longest filled up with meaning. Pregnant an d fecund.
```

view of all that he missed, wasted, didn't partake in
and take advantage of. As the boy and girl commence
their relationship Haberman becomes involved. He too
falls in love, becomes enamored, finds youth and meaning,
his life is once again and for the first time in the
longest filled up with meaning. Pregnant an d fecund.
He dresses differently, youthful, Swatggers when he walks,
rushes home as if in love and he cannot wait to be with his
beleoved.

Then the boy and girl turn the table game on him. They
show themselves to be autonomous, go their own way,
indiffeerent to him, cavoulv so; he the orchestrator
and man repsonbsible for the Robert Habmerman tv show, is
now losing control. The boy and girl don't need him. They
are playing with him. Manipulating him. They like he
before, cpast, manipulate, invent, and produce
their own version of relationship. He is left out. No
longer the orchestrator and producer but someone who is merel-
ly left to watch, not partake, observe passivley rather
than before. He decides to get even. They shot him
out. Barring of TV Scenes (amy work.
He decides to get even. This is a war and all is to be
same fair in love and war. Haberman fights for his life.
He will not be beat out or left out by the boy and girl.
It is his show, his romance, his beleoved, aand by the end
he will take away tthta which he has built, given. He
will destroy the relatonship. The boy and girl, puppets
of his imagination, fight for their very lives. Haberman
tTheir autonomy and contempruosness and a decrepit
old man. Burngt out andindtent. Another generation
hanging on too long, of no use to anybody buhimself.
AS Habemran and the boy and girl fight for thir very
existence, confront eachother, the show, the Pbort Habmerman
show, takes on new meaning. From soap opera to melodrama,
TFrom comedy to deathly seriousness; the game has life
and endeath meaning. Who will win? How far will the contestants go? Will Haberman at the risk of ggiving up
the show, ending the show, ruining the show, destroy the
boy and girl? Will they move out of his apamtment, risk
losing their set and situation in life, the basis and
foundation for their relatonshiop. They too watch television
LIve their lives through tv...or can only relate as Haber-

stable and secure enviornments 214-3

man, through the mechanistic machinations of tv. Will they
leave, end up alone, destroy, forsake haberman. A
battle is waged. The stakes are high. This is a program
The Robert Haberman Show for the age. Will it end in
fyailure, traged, comedy, will it rise above all problems
even when the tv is shut finally shut off to be renewew by a
a new character. A new boy and girl who Haberman might
ginfind in the street one last day to begin again. Will
realtionshpp only begin when the tv is shut off. When all
is dark and quite and we have no more images cloging our
mind. Flashing thorgh our living rooms. When wae are
once agin alone together, in the quiet of the night,
when we can hear each other speak again. Without tv commercial
commericals, interruptions, sounds and noises from the
stretet, and the many other distractions of modern man
coming to hnder and prevent us from dong so.

Sub Plot: As the old man's programs become increasingly
more violent, inducing more and more 'hurt and punishment
upon the youngsters, as the yougsters retaliate in their
Mind, the program Robert Haberman Show becomes more an
and more compreliing, a mfatter of life and death until
the contestants, the prime characters, the boy and girl
and the old man are veritably in a life and death struggle
for survival, the landlord of the building which is the
set for the show has decided to take his comproperty
cooperative. Thus Haberman will have to get out, move,
He has No NO EVICTION CLAUSE or so he thougnt. He has
doesn't have a-no eviction clause and he has to move.
His show will be interrupted. He could never find another
apartment, studio, like this. the boy and girl will
leave him for ever. Something has tto to be done qquickck-
ly he muses. A lfife and death anfd fisnish. A last
knock chance knockout with the one big punch. Life, the
landlord, losing the aprtment, hve necedssited Haberman
take a chance. this last chance. He too is subject to
contingency. the laws beyond the clostered room.

At the end, with the tv screen blank, the room dark,
the images gone once and for all, gone, he muses, maybe
now, with no distractions, sounds, images, tv sets
blasting away, the boy and girl, he hae a chance, a reaL
CHANCE AT RELATIONSHIOP.

        - You are Mr. Kalich's literary agent,
    Svetlana Paccher?

The things one conjures in one's mind when watching the
boy and girl on screen.

        - I was more Mr. Kalich's translator and
    editor than agent when I resided in New
    York. Even in those years his books hardly
    sold.

The things one is capable of.

        - You've read this present text of Mr.
    Kalich's?

        - I'm about halfway through, page 145, to
    be exact.

        - What are your impressions so far?

        - In what capacity: translator? editor?
    agent?

        - Your choice, Ms. Paccher.

        - Well, as a translator I would have to
    say this book is especially difficult

to interpret, being somewhere between reality and fiction. Sometimes even I can't distinguish between what's real and what's not.

- But you are a translator.

- Of course, and in that capacity I can take liberties with Mr. Kalich's prose. The author's language is not etched in stone, you understand. It's a matter of interpretation. Especially for a writer like Kalich.

- Why especially for a writer like Kalich?

- Because for him the act of writing has always been a torture chamber. It's a constant struggle to get the right words out.

- Not that different than a translator?

- Same thing. Yes. Similar.

- And your impressions of the boy and girl?

- To be honest, I'm a little disappointed
he hasn't developed the boy and girl
more. They seem rather flat, passive,
unidimensional. Of course I realize that's
probably the point; that they're meant to
be no more than representations in the
character's mind, much like he sees them
on the television screen, but still, I
would have liked a richer depiction.

- Ms. Paccher, as interesting as your
interpretations of Mr. Kalich's technical
proficiency as an author might be, and as
you've known the man for fifteen to twenty
years now, and have at least in part perused
his book, I'd much prefer to hear your
opinion as to whether Mr. Kalich could have
in some way been responsible for the boy and
girl's suicide.

- First off, I haven't spent any real time
with Mr. Kalich in about ten to twelve
years, since setting up my own agency in
Paris. And he stopped writing, at least I
thought he did.

- And secondly?

- Secondly, before I answer your question,

in all fairness to Mr. Kalich, I'd like to finish reading the book.

- Ms. Paccher, we're pressed for time. I'd appreciate it very much if you could at least venture an opinion.

- Well I don't know if this will help in your assessment, but I will tell you that in the past I've always advised Mr. Kalich not to lose his edge.

- His edge?

- Not to become too comfortable. His misery and anger...it's what fuels his writing. One thing is for certain: without it he wouldn't write the books he does.

- And if he lost it? Or more specifically, if he couldn't write at all: then what?

- That's one book I wouldn't want to translate much less interpret.

Ms. Paccher had already stepped down when she turned to complete her final thought.

```
- You realize when all is said and done,
whether I'm serving in the role of agent,
editor or translator, at bottom, I'm just
a reader like everybody else.
```

Like any good dramatist, once the boy and girl asserted their need for autonomy, I raised the stakes. After all, more important than anything else, I wanted to keep the game interesting.

Now, what would prove most interesting?

a. Create a Love Triangle by inviting a temptress to stay with us in PH-F.

b. Raise the rent to the point where the boy cannot afford to pay. (Threaten to do so again and again.)

c. Set Curfew Hours:

9:00 p.m. on weekdays for the girl

10:00 p.m. on weekdays for the boy.

11:00 p.m. on weekends for both.

d. Impose a No Fraternization Rule: except for those hours when I can supervise and oversee the boy and girl's meetings.

e. All Shopping cancelled.

f. All Luncheons and Dinners cancelled.

g. Impose, as much as feasible, a Social Isolation Rule between the boy and girl in PH-F (and out?)

h. Impose a No Talking Rule.

Naturally The Rules of My Game were designed to provoke the boy and girl to such extremes of violent emotion as to allow them to break through the boundaries of quotidian existence. By setting the proper mood, staging the correct environs, programming the fitting dramaturgy, I would in effect be creating the ideal situation for the boy and girl to realize their fullest possibilities. And, of course, if the boy and girl reached those exalted heights, by my being there to observe them on screen—so would I.

```
- But surely, Mr. Kalich, you must admit
there was an element of cruelty in your
so-called "play."

- All play contains elements of cruelty.
Observe any child at play and you'll
understand what I mean.
```

Ever since I invited the Dance Hall Woman to stay with us in PH-F, the girl hides away in her room; or, if she does come out, mopes around, an anxious, bewildered look on her face.

> - And the fact that the girl slept until
> the third ring of the alarm clock, and
> sometimes never even left her bed all day:
> didn't that tell you something? Mr. Kalich?

Mute, silent, speechless, the girl's world is shattered, her inviolable faith and belief in the boy and myself a thing of the past.

> - You yourself said she reverted to type;
> became virtually catatonic, as she had been
> when first placed in the halfway house.

Her perfect world changed forever by the Dance Hall Woman with the clear cruel eyes, who possesses the full arsenal of female charms and wares. Who possesses all the girl does not.

> - Mr. Kalich, didn't it occur to you that
> you had gone too far with your games?
> That you had gone well beyond the girl's
> endurance?

Of course, I prolong the agony by inviting the woman to stay not just for a weekend as I had originally promised, but for an indeterminate period of time.

> - Or was that the purpose of your game to begin with?

The girl can hardly muster up courage to ask me: How long is the Dance Hall Woman going to stay?

> - And the manner in which the boy was attracted to the woman...

> - You don't mean to hold me responsible for their mutual attraction, do you?

The boy stands as if mesmerized, a strange white pallor frozen on his face, whenever the woman saunters by. Her bosom and cleavage on display, perfume scent trailing her every movement. Needless to say the Dance Hall Woman knows her art well.

> - Mr. Kalich, surely you realized how the boy would be tempted by such a woman.

> - Who can really know what takes place between a man and a woman.

Best of all, and not because of my own encouragements, the Dance Hall Woman truly likes the boy, appreciates his youth and innocence, is flattered by his virginal attentions.

        - And the girl, if only by the boy's
        sudden lapse of interest, she had to know
        what was going on.

        - ...(Enough to cause a rent in her heart
        that would never heal.)

Not only do I ask the girl's permission, but I allow her to make the decision: Should the Dance Hall Woman stay or leave? But please remember, dear girl, the poor woman has no place to go. No money, no friends, no relatives to take her in. And her lover only threatened her with more violence if she were to return. So what do you think? Should we put her on the street or let her stay? But you better than most knows what that would mean. There are no cashmere blankets and rooms fragrant with Chanel on the street, not to mention people such as the boy and myself to love you.

        - I agree.

And then one day the Dance Hall Woman is gone. To heal the wounds between the boy and girl will require much work and who better than I to provide such counsel. My constant maxim: Forgiveness. The flesh is weak. All relationships require work, have their ups and downs, one can hardly blame the boy, or oneself even. After all, he's only human and the woman, of course, was a true goddess, as if sent down from the heavens with but one purpose in mind. Besides, all men are the same. Time immemorial women have had to live with that.

- You agree?

- Yes. Like everything else, sooner or later, all games must come to an end.

Marriage broker, divorce counselor, love therapist and healer, by whim or necessity, I provide wise counsel to both the boy and girl.

I have obsessed over the boy and girl now for a period in excess of twenty-five years. Who's to say which is more real. What I originally imagined for my aborted novel in print, or what I today make happen and observe on screen. Either way the question seems rhetorical. The images of the boy and girl never leave me.

- My apology for calling you back, Mr. Kalich, but as Richard's twin brother

154

you are more qualified to answer these
questions than any other.

- I understand.

Fernando, the concierge, calls me "Mr. K" when I enter or
leave the building. Big George lets out a loud "Kaliiiich!"
Rudy, at the front door, says "Si Señor." And that pretty
much sums up the better part of my social life and connec-
tion with people throughout my so-called golden years.

- You brought to our attention earlier,
Mr. Kalich, that your brother was always a
despairing, forlorn and angry person.

- That's true. Due to the difficulties of
his profession.

- And at the present time, with the
complete collapse of the literary culture,
would it be fair to surmise he might have
become more angry, violent even?

- It depends upon what you mean by violent.

- But then, when the boy and girl came
into his life, he seemed to have changed.

- For the better, I agree.

- But those last several months with the boy and girl, he changed once again; becoming angrier, more violent...

- He might have had good reason.

- Ruthless even.

- Do you have a question?

- Is your twin brother, Mr. Kalich, capable of conducting experiments on the boy and girl to test their reactions, and performing measured dosages of punishments calibrated merely for the sake of exploring various kinds of scientific hypotheses?

The twin remains silent.

- Mr. Kalich, if you would answer the question.

- I told you earlier.

- What did you tell us earlier, Mr. Kalich?

       - My twin brother never shared that part
       of his life with me.

Ever since I raised the stakes when the boy and girl began
to assert their autonomy, I notice I haven't patted any children on the head in the elevator. Interesting: do the boy
and girl affect me as much or more as I, who am making
every effort, do them?

       - If it were merely sex I wanted, I could
       have gone to any prostitute.

       - Then what did you want?

       - It had nothing to do with that.

       - Then what did it have to do with?

Even I was surprised when a locksmith I had occasion to
employ but once was called by the Interrogator.

       - Mr. Mondale, didn't it occur to you
       that by installing the locks you were
       in effect giving Mr. Kalich the license
       to lock the boy and girl into their
       respective rooms?

- No. Why should it? I thought he probably had some kind of valuables in the rooms. Besides, it was none of my business. Mr. Kalich paid me to do a job and I did it. Simple as that.

- When you installed the locks, Mr. Mondale, were the boy and girl in the apartment?

- Not the boy, but I did see the girl in her room.

- Didn't she object?

- No.

- How did she seem?

- Sad, out of it.

- Sad?

- Actually, when I think about it, she looked really beautiful, wearing a white dress.

The ugly woman in 4D hasn't looked up at me once in the elevator since taking up residence in the building at least fifteen years ago, much less said a word. Today I made an especial effort to entice a word or two out of her when I said "Good morning," and then later, that evening, with a theatrical flourish, "Good night." My salutations achieved their desired effect. As she hurried out of the elevator this evening, ostensibly more uncomfortable than ever, she responded by mumbling an indistinct incantation of her own.

- Twice a week, on Mondays and Fridays, the boy and girl would come downstairs to my apartment to hear me read Shakespeare.

- Shakespeare?

- Yes. From our chance meetings on the elevator, Mr. Kalich must have overheard I wanted to be an actor and was in college studying musical theater.

- But you just said Shakespeare. Was classical drama something you were interested in as well as musical theater?

- To tell the truth, Shakespeare bored the hell out of me.

- And yet you maintain Mr. Kalich encouraged the boy and girl to visit your apartment to hear you read Shakespeare?

- Romeo and Juliet specifically.

- Still...

- Well, he never said it in so many words, but I always had the feeling he knew they were sneaking down to my place.

- And how did you arrive at that conclusion?

- He bought them the Romeo and Juliet plays for one. And then the boy and girl visited every Monday and Friday night when Mr. Kalich would go shopping after their dinner meal.

- Mr. Koppel, everybody goes shopping once or twice a week.

- Yeah, but not everybody unlocks certain doors in their apartment when they do so.

- And you're certain Mr. Kalich knew you would be reading Romeo and Juliet to them?

- I doubt he was sending them down to hear me sing Broadway show tunes. He wasn't the type.

- Mr. Koppel, this is a serious matter.

- I know that.

- Why would you do such a thing?

The youth remains silent.

- What I mean to say: by your own admission, you were bored by the Bard; why would you take it upon yourself to read one of his works to the boy and girl?

- I could say it was because I felt sorry for them, being locked up all week long in that concentration camp, but the truth is I had a crush on the girl.

- And can you additionally tell us how the boy and girl responded when you read Romeo and Juliet to them?

- Well, they were no geniuses, that's for sure, but anyone could see what it meant to them. They were really into it.

- How were they into it?

- The girl would wear her white dress like Juliet, and then mouth her lines as I read them. She was really beautiful.

- And the boy?

- He would do the same, never once taking his eyes off Juliet...I mean the girl. Anyway, I have to admit, after a while I began to enjoy it, too. I mean they were really good guys and I was happy to do it for them. Besides, there was one thing more important than anything else.

- And what was that one thing more important than anything else?

- Like Romeo and Juliet, the boy and girl were in love.

Circumstantial testimony or not, this interrogation is not proceeding as I anticipated.

- Mr. Yalkowski, you are a lawyer by profession?

- A retired lawyer. I retired eleven years ago when my wife died.

- And you are friends with the person in question.

- I've known Kalich since we attended City College together.

- And you've socialized with him over the years, visited his penthouse apartment?

- Yes. Many times.

- That includes when the boy and girl resided with him?

- I always told him that wasn't a good idea.

- But you did visit him at that time?

- If I did, I never saw them, not once, directly, but I knew they were there.

- How did you know they were there?

- Because Kalich was watching them on a TV monitor.

- And when your friend asked you to watch
with him, according to your past testimony,
I understand you simply refused.

- Whatever he was doing with the boy and
girl, I didn't want to know. I told him
that more than once.

- But still you...

- I even asked him to go with me to some
Asian massage parlors. But, of course, he
didn't. He would never leave that screen.

- Would you venture an opinion as to why
he was so obsessed?

- I don't know. I saw it for what it was.

- And what was that?

- An old man trying to have some fun.
Make the most of what was left to him in
this world. It was all in his head like
everything else about him.

- So you're saying for Mr. Kalich it was
real, but not for you.

- That's never been a problem for me.

- What's never been a problem for you?

- Knowing what's real or not.

- Like your Asian massage parlors.

- One thing I will say: I always thought
Kalich capable of anything.

Not a gold watch, but seven hundred and fifty paycheck
stubs is what I have to show from my job as caseworker
for the Human Resources Administration, a period spanning thirty-one years, from February 5, 1961 to March
21, 1992. I collected and religiously saved the paycheck
stubs which now lay stashed away somewhere in my kitch-
en cabinet, in two U.S. Post Office Priority envelopes, all
rubber-banded in fine, neat, well-ordered piles and in perfect chronological order. When I quit the job—always a
matter of "next year"—my intent was to use the stubs as
wallpaper for my bathroom walls.

Today I ask: What am I going to do with them?

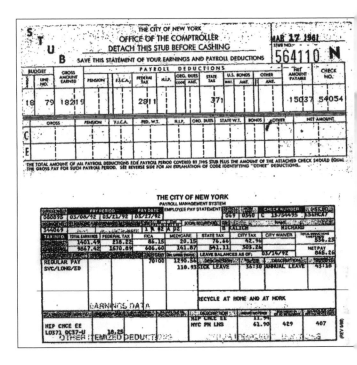

- Is this statement really worth
repeating, Mr. Kalich?

- I think so.

- If you must.

- The two things I had the most capacity for in my life, loving a woman and writing fiction, were the two things which terrified me most.

THE FIVE SENSES RULES

1. TOUCH

2. SIGHT

3. TASTE

4. SMELL

5. HEARING

1. TOUCH: Without exception, all expression(s) of physical intimacy (sex, touch, anything tactile) is not allowed.

2. SIGHT: Though the boy and girl will be permitted to dine at the same table for their one evening meal a day, they will not be allowed to gaze at or even set eyes on one another. Strict adherence to this rule is mandatory and if one or the other (or both) makes an effort to gaze into the other's eyes, or as much as looks up,

both will be deemed culpable and returned to their respective rooms. The same is true if they pass each other in the corridor or any other nook and cranny of PH-F. An air of inviolable correctness is what I'm after, and, as they well know by now, my eyes are all-seeing, and when it comes to my Five Senses Rules, I am particularly unyielding on all counts.

3. TASTE: To be sure, this has nothing to do with culinary appetites, at least not completely, one meal a day is sufficient punishment; but rather is more a corollary of "touch." At any rate, kissing will no more be tolerated than any other physical expression of intimacy.

4. SMELL: The fragrant aroma of Chanel from the girl's room permeates PH-F and with the help of well-placed fans wafts its way to the boy's room. As for his own very masculine musk cologne scent, in similar fashion, that too penetrates the girl's room. Consequently, by smell and hearing the pair remain cognizant of each other. I have to confess, watching the two sniff and smell each other like two feral beasts brings a smile to my countenance; but of course to maximize my pleasure and unlike their four-legged brethren, I never permit them to consummate their passion. Like a zoo-keeper, prison warden or Kommandant of a camp, I rule over my PH-F domain with absolute authority.

5. HEARING: The boy and girl are of course not allowed to speak to each other. For example, not a word is permitted at the dinner table. And if so much as a single word is uttered by either of them, like with sight, it is easy enough to correct the problem by holding one or the other or both accountable, and immediately sending them back to their respective rooms. By way of extension and as a kind of extra-curricular activity, I have installed special high-intensity microphones in the boy and girl's rooms, allowing them to hear every sound made by the other. Thus the boy can hear the girl's inchoate streams of lament, sobs, moans, groans and sighs, and the girl likewise hears every rant, rave and apocryphal sally of the boy's. I can even prolong such emotive sounds depending upon my whim and mood. But, of course, if either or both attempt to bypass my code of silence and take advantage and exploit my microphone sound system by making purposeful sounds of their own, whether they be in words or any other codified language such as a click of the teeth or tongue, a tap or knock of the fingers, knuckles, hands on the hardwood floor, or head against the wall, I immediately shut off the sound system and consign each to impenetrable silence. Like everything else in PH-F, it lies solely in my purview to decide what sounds I let pass through these walls.

- You are Patricia Phillips?

- That is my professional name.

- You are a concert producer?

- After I left my husband I had no choice but to try and make a living. I had a mentally challenged child to support.

- And you knew Mr. Kalich before you established yourself professionally?

- His brother and I dated when we were at NYU.

- And knowing Mr. Kalich as long as you have: do you think him capable of being responsible for the boy and girl's suicide?

- No. He would never cause harm to any young people. Dickie's a sweetie pie.

It's been almost a month now since the boy and girl peered up when dining at the same table; said a word to each other; physically had the slightest contact. They're both so famished and hungry with cravings and needs I can only wonder how this will end.

- On what basis do you suggest Mr. Kalich is a sweetie pie?

- Because of the way he related to my son, Dwight.

- What way was that?

- Dwight was born with certain neurological limitations and Dickie, Mr. Kalich, was the only one of all my friends who embraced him: took him to the park, ball games, movies. If you would have seen them together, you wouldn't even ask such a question.

- Are you saying Mr. Kalich had a similar relationship with the...

- He probably had a soft spot in his heart for the boy and girl just as he did for Dwight. I'll always love Dickie for that.

The last thing I want is for them to lose all hope. What fun would my games be for me or anyone else then.

- You do realize Mr. Kalich's motives weren't altogether altruistic. He did model one of his novel's characters after your son.

- He's a writer. Writers do that sort of thing.

- And that includes his never going anywhere or doing anything.

- I've always said he was different. He didn't have the time to change his socks. He used the backs of his used scrap paper to write on. He had no time. He needed to think...read...write.

- And his living like a hermit?

- He always had his twin brother. And books. He didn't need anybody. That's why he never got married. As long as I knew him he was never lonely. He lived in his own world. Led a secret life. Had his own thoughts and dismissed all the rest.

- In appreciation of the fact that you've read his current work, Ms. Phillips, would you say Mr. Kalich lived in his own world

or created his own world? There is a
difference, Ms. Phillips.

- I've read the book three times and still
don't know what it means. Real or fiction.
It's not the person I know.

- Let me put it another way, Ms. Phillips.
Did Mr. Kalich imagine the boy and girl or
are they real?

- Oh, I don't know. It's all so
complicated. Confusing.

Still, as interesting and amusing as my Five Senses Rules
have proven to be, it's not enough. My mind keeps stir-
ring. My response is not wholly unexpected. What else is
play other than exploring variations on the theme.

- Even Mr. Kalich's brother says he was
always frustrated. Angry.

The concert producer passes a look of mock disap-
proval.

- Ms. Phillips...

- It's not easy being a writer in today's world.

- Ms. Phillips, in all the years wasn't there at least one incident where you saw evidence of this anger?

- Evidence?

- Of another Mr. Kalich. One different than the one you describe with your son.

- Well, there was one time.

- One time?

And so, like a yo-yo, I reverse the procedures of my Five Senses Rules. All I previously denied the boy and girl I now will give. Perhaps a bit too much.

- I had called him to explain why I couldn't speak on the phone to him the night before when I was with people at a restaurant, rushing through dinner to get to my friend Donny's show, which was being reviewed that night by the NY Times.

- And...?

- And when he heard the NY Times, he exploded.

- Exploded. How?

- He was furious, screaming how he couldn't get his own books reviewed even though a NY Times literary critic lived in his building, and how, in order to avoid confronting him, she would hide in the mailroom when seeing him in the lobby, or turn her back to him in the elevator, standing like a naughty six-year-old in school in the corner, staring at the wall, and this hack, this mediocrity, my friend Donny—he called him a Catskill Mountain comic, not a playwright but an entertainer, the lowest level, banality, not Eugene O'Neil but Jackie Mason. It was terrible. His rampage came as if from nowhere. I was stunned. Shocked.

- Taking this rampage into consideration, Ms. Phillips, do you still consider Mr. Kalich a sweetie pie incapable of being responsible for the boy and girl's suicide?

- Oh, I don't know. One thing has nothing to do with the other.

Everybody knows what's taken place in PH-F. People in the building have been privy to the rumors and innuendoes for the longest time. In fact, most have probably seen the ravaged and war-torn bodies of the boy and girl firsthand. Certainly the ROMEO AND JULIET SUICIDE has been well publicized in the newspapers, media, TV and Internet. And yet not a word, not a glance in my direction from the good citizens. One would think, at the very least, mothers chronically protective of their children would guard them all the closer in my presence. Would speak in whispers, walk on tiptoes, take the little ones' hands, prod them toward their skirts, push them out the elevator door more quickly, or hasten their step when walking through the lobby corridors. But no, not true; to the residents, staff, friends and neighbors of my building, I am as invisible as ever.

Is it sheer callousness, indifference, or something else?

Whatever.

THE FIVE SENSES RULES (revised)

1. TOUCH: Like a virtual reality designer, I clothe the boy and girl in bodysuits. Hands, mouths, feet, all sexual parts insulated by layers of rubber fabric. They know the rules: They can caress and hug each other

as much as they want, to their hearts' content, but the bodysuits must stay on. Famished and hungry as they are, desperate for contact, any physical intimacy, they make every effort to touch and fondle, embrace and paw, stimulate and bring each other pleasure. All their efforts are in vain. The only one finding any pleasure here is myself, sitting comfortably in front of my TV screen. And it's not mere fantasy I experience, but lust. So much so, I can hardly contain myself as I watch the histrionics and gyrations of the twosome on screen. My only concern is that my laughter and change of mood will be noted outside PH-F. But even that doesn't bother me too greatly. For as stated, nobody really cares what goes on behind these walls.

- Mr. Korman, as a childhood friend of Mr. Kalich, one who goes even further back than Ms. Phillips, are you in accord with what she said?

- As children they were different.

- How were they different?

- They didn't need other kids.

- Could you elaborate?

177

- You know how other kids need each other for confirmation. Validation. The Kalich twins didn't. They had each other.

I notice that I continue to rely as much on my aborted novel's voluminous pages as I do on my own imagination for conjuring up ideas for my Five Senses Rules. To that end, as we're having an early and exceptionally harsh winter this year, I wrap myself in my quilt blanket, fluff my pillows, and, like a sickly child waiting for his mother's hot soup, I snuggle in bed to peruse my notes. These bedtime hours have the added advantage of allowing me to get away for an hour or two from the burden of having either to listen to others or myself answer difficult questions on the part of the Interrogator. I must admit, rereading my notes and contemplating the various games envisioned affords me significant pleasure. But truly nothing can compare to the perfect moments bordering on ecstasy I receive from the actual implementation and watching of the boy and girl's responses to my well-conceived and executed games.

Now, what game shall I/we play?

I must never forget the adage: One receives from an experience what one brings to it. Who is that more true for than myself?

- Not all my games are the same.

- You freely admit that?

Sometimes one has to sacrifice grace and charm for the sake of results. It is not inconceivable that some might call several of my choices crude.

- Most definitely. But far more salient
here, I would emphasize, is the fact that
not once, no matter how powerful and crude
my games were, did I ever lay hands on the
boy and girl.

- Not once?

- Not once.

Sometimes one sense readily combines with another to make for an especially amusing game. Such is the case with Sight and Hearing, or should I say Sight and Sound, if only because the conjunction is more sonorous.

2 & 3. SIGHT & SOUND: I have two muscle-bound, bald-headed men, much resembling eunuchs on loan from some mid-century fiefdom, escort a particularly

attractive young woman and young man past the boy and girl's respective rooms. As if by accident, their doors have been left slightly ajar so that they can gain a glimpse of the attractive youths. Soon enough, with a click of my fingers I shut the lights off leaving the boy and girl not only in pitch black rooms, but alone with their imaginations. Next I tunnel into their rooms amatory sounds I recorded of the pair making love to each other from earlier encounters, now separated and isolated with the aid of a highly skilled sound engineer. The boy can hear the girl's sighs, moans, groans; her "oh yeah, I like it. Good. It feels so good...please don't stop...don't come...please..." And the girl in turn hears the boy's aggressive hard-edged male thrusts and lusty harangue: "Like this?...how's it feel?...now you... yeah...that's it...that's good...yeah...oh yeaaaaah!" But neither of the two can know for certain who or what is prompting such love sounds from the other. They can only imagine, call forth their darkest fears. And, if it's true, and I, for one, believe it is, that we receive from an experience what we bring to it—I am most fortunate that I don't even have to imagine what the boy and girl are bringing/thinking. I know: delusional unstable minds, passive wills, weak senses of self, inability to distinguish reality from fantasy, in short and in sum, the accumulated baggage of their lifetimes.

The mind is a terrible thing to waste our contemporary sages tell us, and, for my purposes, I would venture a guess that I, an emblematic figure of conservationism, am making the best possible use of these two minds.

- Even though you couldn't write
your novel, "Transfiguration of the
Commonplace," Mr. Kalich, you say you knew
how it would end?

- Yes. That's my particular gift and
what's so frustrating. As I've repeatedly
said, I see my novels whole, beginning,
middle and end, and at the same time I...

- Because of other problems you still
couldn't write it.

- Precisely. That's why I invited the boy
and girl into PH-F in the first place.

- Mr. Kalich, I feel compelled to ask
you, in addition to being able to see
your novels whole, did you also see your
relationship with the boy and girl whole?

- I don't understand the question.

- In other words, Mr. Kalich, is it
possible that even before taking the boy
and girl into PH-F, you already knew how
your relationship with them would end?

NOTES...THE TRANSFIGURATION OF THE COMMONPLACE

END: 10/24/1985

A man and woman tied together at the waist, joined at the
hip, jump from their apartment on West 66th St...Could this
be my ending? Romeo and Juliet?

****10/24/85
      6/19/05   20 Years!!!

         9/12/2006

- And to that end you purposefully left
their doors unlocked, allowing them to
visit the young actor.

- Even prison inmates and other
institutionalized people are given an hour
or two to themselves to walk the yard,
grounds or garden as the case may be.

- Where he would read to them passages of
Romeo and Juliet.

- They were very much taken by the characters.

- More than taken, they were highly impressionable, vulnerable, it might even be fair to say that the boy and girl wholly identified with Shakespeare's lovers.

- Surely, Mr. Kalich, you didn't purchase tickets for the boy and girl to attend the Romeo and Juliet play so far in advance merely for the sake of entertainment.

- As you yourself have mentioned, the boy and girl have always expressed an affinity for Shakespeare's lovers.

- But why so far in advance? The play never even approached selling out.

Not a word out of Kalich.

- One can only conclude that your wanting the boy and girl to see the play was integral to another agenda you had in mind long before.

Sometimes an idea occurs to me which is so appealing I cannot resist even if it means repeating a sense that I've already explored; although, of course, in a different way. Such is the case with...

1A. TOUCH: And so in the spirit of Christmas I offer the boy and girl complete freedom to do with each other what they want. For as long as they want. In total privacy, with nobody there to bother them, least of all myself. My terrace is for them and them alone. Of course eleven inches of snow, single digit temperatures, and ice cold penetrating winds will accompany them outdoors. But the view is magnificent, overlooking Central Park, and, well, after all, it is a white Christmas. What true lovers could resist? Once they're outside, I rest on my laurels, sit back with a hot cocoa in hand and observe the pair on screen. The poor dears: matted together, limbs shivering, lips blue, I can hear their teeth chattering. Do they even have shoes on? One can only guess as to how long love can endure in such circumstances. To be honest, I was more than pleasantly surprised as their long distance efforts only prolonged my own tears of joy and laughter.

"Merry Christmas! Joy to the world!" I shouted as I opened the terrace doors letting the boy and girl reenter my apartment and join me. Other than their chattering teeth and an almost audible shivering, they both seemed incapable of uttering a sound. They didn't even look like human beings anymore, standing there like frozen slabs of meat already shrunken in size, spoiled and rotted. A strange erotic excitement I had not known for the longest time overtook me as I commenced vigorously rubbing the girl's feet like my mother would do when, as children, my twin and I would return home from sleigh-riding jaunts on Riverside Drive. An even greater sense of power and erotic command enveloped me as I observed the girl's imploring, pleading eyes begging that I do the same for the boy, who continued standing stoically at her side, asking nothing for himself, but rather only for the girl. As I started rubbing the boy's feet I surmised, as with the rich and powerful, one's generosity is all the more satisfying when one holds the purse strings.

Finishing up with the boy's feet, and before sending each to their respective rooms, I whispered in urgent tones: "Whatever possessed you two to go outdoors on a night like this?"

But why then, after such a pleasant and amusing game would I not sleep that night? Two images kept recurring in my mind. The boy's stoical refusal of my help and the girl's imploring, pleading eyes that had her lover's welfare more selflessly in mind than her own. At such moments in the middle of the night, drenched in sweat that made my skin stick to the sheets, and simultaneous with the images,

I kept hearing for the second time in my life a little voice emanating from somewhere deep inside me saying: Who's going to love me? Who's going to love me? Along with the added proviso—like Romeo and Juliet love each other?

The next morning my resolve to play with the boy and girl and subject them to even more punishing tests and trials was all the stronger.

- You refer to your activities with the boy and girl as mere games, Mr. Kalich, play if you will, but aren't they in actuality more like tests, trials, more often than not even cruel punishments?

- How many times are you going to persist in asking the same question?

- How many times are you going to persist in giving the same answer?

The Interrogator, too, can play games.

- And while watching the boy and girl on your TV monitor you admit, Mr. Kalich, to being transported to another state of being?

- One could say that.

- So much so that the boy and girl no longer seemed human to you, not even real.

- ...Unconditional surrender, abject submission...

- What was that?

Vigorously, I shake my head.

- Nothing.

- And so it was that you created the proper environment and played your games?

I remain silent.

- Mr. Kalich, if it was in you as a novelist, it was in you as a man. Even you have to admit that much.

- What I admit is that without my considerable efforts the boy and girl would have come to nothing.

- And you, Mr. Kalich, what have you come to with the boy and girl?

And...

- You say, Mr. Kalich, that if not for you the boy and girl would never have known love.

- It was I who brought them together.

- One might say they did something similar for you.

- What are you suggesting?

- Your greatest fear perhaps was that you would lose them. That they would no longer need you and move out of PH-F on their own.

- They could never do that.

- But if they could?

- As I've already said: Every game has to end.

And this from a fellow writer and long-term friend.

- You met Mr. Kalich for brunch for a period spanning eighteen years?

- Yes. Every Sunday like clockwork we would meet at Fairway's restaurant at 11:00 a.m.

- And then suddenly you stopped. Can you tell me why?

- There were many reasons.

- Can you start with one?

- He was always angry; constantly roasting me and saying the same things.

- Same things?

- Actually one: "Literature ruined my life!"

- And that was the reason...

- It was like a recitativo.

- ...you stopped going to brunch with him?

- No. Not only that. I'm a writer, too. I could identify with that.

- Well, what else then?

- He would project his own bitterness and misery onto me.

- How did he do that?

- He would constantly berate my work saying I had wasted my life, like he did, with my lyric writing.

- Taking this into...

- And he never really took me seriously as a writer. He was always beleaguering me with the same questions.

- And that was?

- How could I waste my talent on such trivial concerns?

- And despite...

- The truth is more people sing my songs than read his books. If his publishers sold twenty-eight books, it would double the sales of his two books published all over the world.

- And despite all these insults and abuse you continued joining him for brunch?

- I never felt that way about my life. I might not have made much money at my writing, but I had a great psychic income. I once wrote an opera which was produced in Germany. And I co-wrote a musical that...

- Mr. Byron, if you would please stay with the subject.

- Besides, we're different kinds of writers.

- Of course. You're a lyricist and Mr. Kalich is a novelist.

- That's not what I mean.

- What do you mean?

- We had more serious problems than writing. He could be a bastard.

- A ba...?

- There was a time I was having sexual difficulties with my second wife. She was young at the time and I confided in him.

- And?

- He laughed.

- Laughed?

- I knew it was a mistake the second I opened my mouth. He was always more concerned with books than people. And in those later years, life, books, it was all the same to him. Fun and games.

- And as I said, yet you continued...

- He wasn't always like that. When young we had great literary discussions. I was in awe of his talent. He was brilliant. But in these last years he just changed.

- You mean when he took the boy and girl into PH-F?

- The truth is he was harder on himself than anyone else.

192

- And it was about that same time, when
the boy and girl moved into PH-F with him
that you stopped meeting him for brunch...
every Sunday like clockwork at 11:00 a.m.?

- Not me. Him.

- Him?!

- It was actually some years before they
moved in.

- But why?

- It was as if books, literature,
badgering and fulminating against me
was no longer important to him. I guess
without that we just ran out of things to
say to each other.

- Mr. Byron. Once and for all: was Mr.
Kalich capable of being responsible for
the boy and girl's suicide?

The lyricist ponders the question.

- Mr. Byron?

- I don't know how to answer that question except to say: look what he did with his first novel, "The Nihilesthete."

- What did he do?

- When he finished, he brought the manuscript to an editor. The editor didn't believe he was the author.

- Why not?

- He didn't believe that a normal-looking person like Kalich could have written a book so perverse and grotesque.

- But the boy and girl's suicide didn't just take place in his novel.

- I know.

And something similar from another writer; this one young.

- Mr. Belkin. Can you tell us about the screenplay you co-wrote with Mr. Kalich.

- A producer paid us a small advance to collaborate on a horror film. We never completed the script.

- Why not?

- Because Mr. Kalich has no respect for the film medium. Even less so for the horror film genre. Fact is, he disdains it. Over and over I recall him saying to me: You young screenplay writers have no idea what truly great writing is.

- And naturally you don't share his opinions.

- Of course not. I love film. And I enjoy horror films in particular. I pop down my $11.00. I get myself a bag of popcorn and I sit down and enjoy them...like everybody else.

As painstakingly thorough as I am in my pursuits, it seems the Interrogator is equally so.

- I remember because the show was sold out on that particular night and Mr. Kalich had already purchased the last of the good seats available.

- But Mr. Kalich did purchase orchestra seats?

- That's what I'm trying to explain to you. If you'll just allow me to finish.

- Please.

- As I was saying. On that particular night the show had sold out which was very unusual for a Romeo and Juliet play, especially so far in advance, and I won't even try to explain. There are just some nights when that happens.

- Mr. Parker, about Mr. Kalich's ticket purchase.

- Yes. He had already purchased the last of the orchestra seats available and was leaving the ticket window when these two women, the next in line, got in a huff when I told them that all we had available were partial view seats. They were obviously disappointed and started to question me about the seats when, almost inadvertently, I referred to the partial views as "love seats." At least that's what we called them in the old days. Today, just the conventional boxes.

- Mr. Parker...

- Yes. At any rate, from inside my ticket window, at my mere mention of the term "love seats," I couldn't help noticing Mr. Kalich's ears perk up and immediately going up to the women and negotiating an exchange of his orchestra seats for the partial views.

- And you're certain Mr. Kalich had already purchased two orchestra seats for the play?

- Yes. That's why I remember the incident so vividly.

- Mr. Parker, by chance did you additionally happen to overhear any further exchange between Mr. Kalich and the two women that would explain why he would relinquish his two orchestra seats for two partial views?

- As a matter of fact I did. They were standing directly in front of my ticket window and I distinctly heard him say to the women that he was doing it because they were so disappointed, but to be

honest I thought there was something else
involved.

- Like what?

- The way Mr. Kalich insisted, wouldn't
take no for an answer. It just seemed, to
me at least, he really wanted those love
seats.

As with Sight and Sound, Taste and Smell make for a formidable combination.

3 & 4. TASTE & SMELL: I bathe the boy and girl in milk
and honey, or cover each with layers of chocolate ice
cream and syrup. And I let them clean the impasto
from the other's body by making use of their mouths,
lips, tongues, nothing else. Chocolate ice cream and
syrup seems to be their favorite based on time at least:
The boy taking exactly two minutes flat and the girl
two minutes and ten seconds to do the job. As for
milk and honey, comparable times can be expected,
maybe thirty to forty seconds longer than their favorite. Piss, urine, whether it be from animals or humans,
requires, as one would expect, longer periods of time,
but are surprisingly close. Human piss: approximately

seven minutes twenty seconds; animal urine: seven minutes thirty-nine seconds. But with any combination or permutation of animal excrement: turds and shit from dogs, pigeons, cats, squirrels, especially horse manure, the cleaning process can go on ad nauseam. At least it must seem to the boy and girl like forever. For me, of course, it's never long enough. Time, like all the Aristotelian unities in our post-modern world, has been shattered forever.

By the way, their own human waste is in another time zone altogether.

It would be interesting to understand my twin brother's ambivalence towards me and how it corresponds (if it does) to my own inner conflicts.

```
- My brother's always been miserable. From
the time of our bar mitzvah when, under
great stress from our cantor father, who
presided over an old European orthodox
shul, he lost twenty pounds because he
assumed total responsibility for reciting
the liturgy (and I did nothing)...to
when he went to City College and would
```

```
study all night (and I to NYU where I
had nothing but fun)...to the army where
he served in the reserves for six years
(and I avoided by feigning psychological
problems)...and to the two women he loved
both ending up in nervous breakdowns
(whereas I...
```

When twenty-four, I laid in bed for six months crying when the Israeli, Hana, left me; and then walked around New York for two-and-a-half years numb, crazed, in a sleepwalk. Twenty-eight years later, with the young harpist, Dobrinka: four years of misery, torment, not one good day.

```
- If I would have received ten percent of
what he's received as a writer, I'd be the
happiest guy in the world. He's an idiot. So
disconnected...conflicted...torn apart.
```

Two acclaimed novels, "The Nihilesthete" and "Charlie P."

```
- Could never make a decision. Even when
he was young and found his penthouse
apartment on Central Park West with a
terrace overlooking the park, and rent-
control!--he couldn't.
```

Published in eleven countries.

    - He procrastinated forever until he
    nearly lost it.

Praised by the best literary minds.

    - I took one look and told him to grab it.

Awards...

    - No intimacy. Always alone. Half a life.

Honors...

    - A seventy-year-old man worrying about
    his physical appearance. Ridiculous!

Why not enough? Why?

    - My brother's always been miserable since
    we were kids. And it has nothing to do
    with his being a writer or anything else.
    He's just miserable.

When I ask myself what I did with my life, what I accomplished, my answer has always been: the three novels I wrote, two acclaimed; and the two times I experienced love. But at this point I realize my books have little value and my loves were not reciprocal, not mutual, not whole or complete. If anything, they were all in my mind.

When the Interrogator sums it all up, I can only wonder how it will tally. What does it all mean?

Still, there is more to a man than being a social isolate. For example, for four years at City College I was enamored of the beautiful Thea Goldstein and yet too shy to speak to her. Surreptitiously, I trailed after her, jotting down in a special notebook every stitch of clothing she wore. Befriended a member of her clique, whom I literally helped put through the rigors of an academically demanding school, to insure my remaining close to her; and after four years of such distant orphic enchantment, worship even, I learn, when Thea uttered her first words to me at her engagement party in her parents' home in the Bronx, that she had a crush on me all those years. So much so, she exclaimed, that she would draw my picture in her art class.

- You are Rhonda Brooke, formerly known as Rhonda Brookstein, the person Mr. Kalich

202

befriended to secure a close place in Thea Goldstein's life.

- Yes. But he never put me through City College. I did my own work.

- Can you tell us about the engagement party?

- There's nothing to tell.

- By that I mean did your friend, Thea Goldstein, actually have a crush on Mr. Kalich all those years without either of them ever speaking to each other?

- As I said: There's nothing to tell.

- What do you mean there's nothing to tell?

- I mean there was no engagement party. Thea was never engaged while attending City College. And, for sure, she didn't have a so-called crush on Dick Kalich.

- Are you certain there was no engagement party? How can you be so certain?

- Because I was Thea's best friend in those years. I would have been there.

All these years later and I still carry inside me the smile Thea offered me while looking up from a basement window of 7 Steps, a lesbian bar in Greenwich Village.

And similarly I remember one night with Hana when I spread my arms as wide as my young twenty-four-year-old mind could dream and said: "We could have everything."

And not so much envy, or even admiration, but every July I am astounded by a man in the building who packs his wife, two small children and belongings into his station wagon and drives off for their summer vacation.

And Big George who exudes such pride when seated in his Lexus SUV with a license plate reading "CUBA."

Sometimes the last person one would expect, Mel Yalkowski, comes to my aid.

> - From what I saw of Kalich that last time
> in his apartment, I had the feeling he was
> tempted to visit an Asian massage parlor
> with me. Still, he remained obsessed with
> the boy and girl. Whether love or hate or
> some weird amalgam of the two, he would
> never do anything to jeopardize losing
> them.

And, to some extent, even the Israeli, Hana.

> - I had many lovers in my life, but nobody
> ever gave as much of himself to me as
> Dick. Unfortunately, when I met him, I
> already had two children and was a good
> ten years older than him and needed a
> husband.

Six months after the boy and girl's suicide and I still sit in front of my TV screen interpolating from my notes future plottings of the pair on the blank screen.

> - The way he looked at us.

> - And what way was that, Mrs. Baruch?

> - As if my husband and I were vile,
> reptilian creatures.

> - And you insist, Mrs. Baruch, that in
> your more than forty years as residents
> in the building, neither you nor your
> husband, Mr. Baruch, gave Mr. Kalich...

> - And with such hatred. On the elevator he
> would snicker at us.

- ...any good reason to feel this way?

- More than once I heard him talking to Big George about my husband.

- And?

- He called him a concentration camp Jew.

- But Mr. Kalich is himself Jewish?

- And all this hatred, disdain, malignancy for no other reason than we were old...

"I do not believe that death is man's real problem, or that art entirely permeated by it is completely authentic. The real issue is growing old, that aspect of death which we experience daily. Yet not even growing old, and that property of it, the fact that it is so completely, so terribly cut off from beauty. Our gradual dying does not disturb us, it is rather the beauty of life becomes inaccessible to us."

— Witold Gombrowicz,
Diary, 1953

No matter how difficult, the one thing I've learned is that for a few minutes together, the boy and girl will gladly subject themselves to the most merciless of my games. During last month's blizzard, for example, I placed the girl in the farthest reaches of the city, a god-forsaken wasteland not even possessing a name. The boy can have three minutes with the girl if...I repeat...if he can find her. I furnished him only with the borough name and a makeshift map marking where the girl was to be found. Before starting off he had to remove the outer layers of his clothes. At most he was left with a pair of sneakers and socks, cord trousers and a thin short-sleeved summer shirt. To his credit, like a Monopoly game player, as soon as he heard my "go" he was off to the races, while I trailed along in the comforts of a warm luxuriant limo. Studying his makeshift map, asking off-putted strangers for directions, following false leads, climbing over shoulder-high snow drifts, falling all too often on icy streets from cold, exposure and exhaustion, he made his way through the mazes and labyrinths of the city, step by painful step. Finally, almost a full day later, in the early hours of the morning, he found the girl. Wrapped in a threadbare shawl, hiding in a doorway, eyes glazed and dull, weary and beat, she was nearly as frozen as he was, shielding herself as best she could from the cold, wind and snow.

What must their three minutes be like?

One thing is certain: I have never known three minutes like that in my life.

On the ride home, with the boy and girl sitting on each side of me, folded in warm U.S. army issue blankets, rather than feel satisfaction for a game well played, I felt a depth of anger rising in me as I realized that these two have what I never would. Rest assured, even before reaching PH-F I had already availed myself of my next game to test the limits of the boy and girl's love.

Abominable luck! Just when the boy and girl, only a little while ago sitting frozen on each side of me in the car, had found their way to their special place, the boy's room, were already under the blankets, blissfully nestling together, cheek to cheek, their favorite music playing, a warm glow emanating from the woodburning fireplace yours truly had installed, and I, finally was seated comfortably in my TV room, hot cocoa in hand, ready to observe the Grand Guignol Show, my TV screen goes on the blink. Breaks down. I don't have the words to describe how I felt. It was as if my life broke down with it. Or, more accurately, ceased to exist. Trying to fix the TV monitor I cursed my-self for my lack of knowhow and technical ineptitude. At a loss as to what to do, I banged the monitor with my fists. Hit my head against the wall. Cursing and ranting at my bad luck, my ignorance, I felt my knees go weak, my left wrist drain of all energy, my heart hammer against my chest. And as I remained seated in front of the blackened screen, it wasn't long before I was as mute and catatonic as the girl in her worst moments. I couldn't even imagine what the boy and girl were doing. Without the screen to help me I was literally bereft. I had lost my ability to imagine through imaginings.

> - You refer to your activities with the
> boy and girl as mere games, Mr. Kalich,
> play, if you will, but aren't they in fact
> more like tests, trials, more often than
> not even cruel punishments?
>
> - How many times are you going to persist
> in asking the same question?
>
> - How many times are you going to persist
> in giving the same answer?

Walking to the Food Emporium earlier this afternoon, I noticed a beautiful young homeless woman crouched against the building wall. Returning with the groceries I stopped to chat with her. I was right. She is sad, inconsolably sad and alone.

Does this mean I am nearing the end of one chapter and already anticipating starting another?

In that regard I hear San Francisco has a large population of young people and their homeless population is quite large too. And the climate is pleasant all year round.

But, no, there is much yet to do here. I must stay focused. I must not yield. I must not succumb to my fear of closing a book anymore than, as in the past, I succumbed to my fear of starting one.

When I first conceived the boy and girl's rooms to be on opposite sides of the apartment from my own room, I had in mind the medieval castle where a harem girl is held captive and visited by her master who would walk stealthily through the long dungeon corridors lighted by flame lanterns. In a similar fashion I imagined—if the boy and girl wanted to visit each other at night, they would first have to make their way past my room.

Now to reap what I have sown:

I leave the girl's bedroom door unlocked at night. The long corridor is laden with shards of shattered glass, jagged-edged metal fence, glowing coals, razor barbed wire and cauldrons of boiling water. If the boy is to reach her bedroom, he will first have to trespass a veritable obstacle course of pain and difficulty. And when, with torn and bloody feet, crawling like a centipede, he finally does reach his journey's end, opens the door and makes his way to his beloved's bed, what awaits him: naught but an empty bed. The girl is nowhere to be found. On the contrary, she is seated alongside me watching the TV monitor in wide-eyed horror as I turn to her and say: Juliet, do you have any doubt that Romeo dost truly love you?

But my words are just that: words. Veils of flummery. Inwardly I feel as bereft, barren and desolate as the boy must have felt when finding the girl's bed empty. Irregardless of what I might have earlier said or thought, I know now to conquer a love like theirs will never again merely be a game to me. Romeo and Juliet have proven to be more than worthy opponents.

After an especially harsh and pitiless winter where I've subjected the boy and girl to all that I had to give, tested their limits and asked them to endure more than even I had a right to expect, spring has finally arrived. I've gotten in the habit of taking the pair out for a walk in the park these last several weeks. With flowers budding, birds chirping, change, hope, expectancy is in the air, but nowhere is this more apparent than in the boy and girl. I can only compare them to those people who have suffered massive brain trauma and have lost all capacity for spatial and temporal orientation, literally don't know where they are, and yet when seated in a hospital garden, surrounded by nature and greenery, somehow, some way, they become oriented and their world makes sense again. Something similar has happened to the boy and girl. Once outdoors, amidst the park's commotion and din, almost preternaturally, biologically, I've seen the pair come to life. No longer depleted, sickly and defeated, and despite all my remorseless games and trials, once again, as always, the lovers yearn to share their love. Though I would never show my feelings, or admit my disappointment, I know that despite having played my games as well as I can, the boy and girl have survived not only nature's most brutal of winters, but my own man-made version as well.

I have but one last game to play:

The lovers are scheduled to see the play this afternoon. Will their seeing the play be all I hoped for? Who can say? One can only wonder if, like their Romeo and Juliet counterparts, all my accumulated preparations will have the desired effect. As for me this Sunday morning, I've done all that I can. Like a dawn before battle, everything is arranged down to the last detail. The girl's white dress lies on her bed, the boy's jacket, shirt and tie on his. And champagne to celebrate the festive occasion both before they leave for the play and, more importantly, after, upon their return. From this point on everything is up to them. After taking a sip and wishing them well, or should I say adieu, I hurry off. "The Guitar Man of Central Park" is making his first appearance of the new spring season to-day. Coincidence or not, I intend to enjoy the music.

- You are the boy and girl?

The boy and girl nod imperceptibly.

- Did Mr. Kalich cause your double suicide? Or in some way come to influence your double suicide?

The boy and girl nod imperceptibly.

- Prior to your leaving for the play that Sunday morning, Mr. Kalich had already set the champagne glasses on your kitchen table as if for a festive occasion. Can you tell me what the festive occasion was that you were celebrating?

The boy peers at the girl.

- Perhaps it was simply because the day had finally arrived when you were to see the Romeo and Juliet play?

The girl peers at the boy.

- Or was it rather to inaugurate some other far more definitive rite of passage?

Both smile.

- Did the idea of a double suicide originate while you were viewing the stage play or after? Or was the idea put in your heads long before by Mr. Kalich?

Both smile.

- When Mr. Kalich departed for the park that Sunday morning, did he leave you with any parting words?

...

- And, if so, what were those words?

The boy and girl reach out to hold each other's hands.

- In addition to helping you select your
white Juliet dress; permitting you both
to receive readings on the play from
the young actor in the building; and
purchasing tickets for you to attend the
play; what else did Mr. Kalich do to put
the idea of committing a double suicide
like Romeo and Juliet in your heads?

The boy and girl peer at each other.

- Or was it that you were already so
despairing and emotionally spent by that time
that suicide seemed your only viable solution?

The two continue to peer warily at each other.

- When Mr. Kalich observed you both on his
TV monitor, he perceived you as something
less than human, as more unreal than real.
May I ask how you perceived Mr. Kalich?

A knowing smile passes between the two.

- Consequent to perceiving you in this
manner he would take free rein and
trespass, play his hate-crazed games with
you strictly for his own amusement:

...

- Is that a fair assessment?

- Have I left anything out?

The boy and girl hold each other's hands even more tightly.

- In addition to voluntarily sharing your
intimate secrets with Mr. Kalich, as you
well know by now, he observed your most
private moments on his screen. Therefore
I must ask: Was there anything Mr. Kalich
did not know about you two? Did you hold
back anything?

...

- If so, what?

Even I was a bit disarmed when, as already indicated, the girl told me of her preference for oral sex; and the boy confessed how, when living on the street, in a confrontation with another homeless person, his stabbing the waif resulted in the man losing his eye.

- Other than your obvious weakness and depletion, was there any other reason you let Mr. Kalich do with you what he wanted? In other words, if it was all fun and games to him, what did participating in his games mean to you? Or were you two just so far gone and desperate to stay together that you would endure anything?

The boy and girl smile.

- Please try and help me here. Without your cooperation it's outside all our previous experience to really comprehend what took place between you and Mr. Kalich.

The lovers raise their hands to their mouths to suppress a burst of laughter.

There is a difference conjuring up ideas for my aborted novel, "The Transfiguration of the Commonplace," and my actually living the experience with the boy and girl. But what is it? Is it too facile to argue that fiction and reality are the same? At first glance my notes in preparation for the novel seem to perfectly coincide with what I have experienced with the boy and girl. But is that really the case? Do reality and fiction, word and image, truly mesh and merge and become one and the same? For example, am I any closer to answering my greatest fear which is knowing whether the boy and girl are real or imagined, fiction or reality? Perhaps this is not an existential question but rather an epistemological question. Perhaps even a new epistemology is called for in our image-laden world. Be that as it may, possibly, at a later date, I will make a more thorough study and decode the similarities and differences...if there are any. For now though, with this ongoing chapter in my life, it is enough to say that the boy and girl are real.

Interesting how that one little fact so readily slips my mind.

> - Ultimately, how did you two come to
> understand the play? Were you able to
> appreciate it as a work of art? Or did it
> resonate in you in a less abstract, more
> concrete way? And most importantly, would
> either of you, or both, offer an opinion
> as to how seeing Romeo and Juliet on stage
> compared to Mr. Kalich seeing you on screen?

> ...

> - Is that a fair question?

Unable to cover their mouths fast enough, the pair burst into simultaneous peals of laughter.

Flustered, the Interrogator takes a moment before continuing.

- You two have not responded to
one question put before you in this
interrogation. Is there nothing either of
you wish to say or are you simply going to
let your deed speak for itself?

NOTES FROM THE NOVEL: THE TRANSFIGURATION OF THE COMMONPLACE

When he returned home he put on the video monitor but, of
course, as he anticipated, the boy and girl were gone. The
tv screen was blank. Where?...How?...he wondered. All he
knew was that his life was once again as empty as the blank
screen. He asked himself if his greatest fear was true.
Had he imagined the boy and girl? Was his encounter with
them a fiction? Were they even real to begin with or just
figments of his writer's imagination, not unlike the invented characters in his novels. The sharp pain in the middle
of his stomach he awoke with every morning thereafter, no
different than what he had experienced with the Rumanian, Ina,
so many years before, told him that they were. One can't be
certain about such things, but it's dubious whether Haberman
ever watched another tv screen again.

- So, Mr. Kalich, on that Sunday you were
in the park listening to David Ippolito's
music?

- Yes. As I've said more than once, I
anticipated returning to PH-F some time
after the matinee broke which is around
5:00 p.m.

- That's a long time to listen to music.

- He's an exceptionally gifted singer.

- Exceptional or not, Mr. Ippolito had
to cut his concert short as there was a
downpour beginning at three o'clock.

- Yes...

- And yet you still didn't return to PH-F
until well after 4:40 p.m.

- There's more to Central Park than David
Ippolito's music.

- Even when it's raining?

220

- You are Ms. Kumba Katombo?

- Yes.

- You are employed by the Wexner family as a nanny to care for their three-year-old daughter?

- Yes.

- And you know Mr. Kalich?

- Yes. Mr. Kalich is a nice man. Polite. He always holds the door for me and asks how I am and how my little girl is.

- And on the Sunday in question, Ms. Katombo, you're certain that it was at precisely 4:40 p.m. when Mr. Kalich suddenly ended his conversation in the park with you and hurried off?

- Yes.

- How can you be so certain of the time?

- Because every day at exactly 4:25 p.m. I take the dog for a walk, and that Sunday

was no exception. As soon as he made
his telephone call on his cell phone and
nobody answered...I tell you for an old
man Mr. Kalich ran off like the wind.

   Ms. Katombo breaks into a wide grin.

Every time I visited Dobrinka at her apartment only a few
blocks from mine I would never walk, but would quicken
my step to double-time. I could never wait to get there.

The same with Hana: Whenever she would ask me to fetch
cigarettes for her on the lobby floor I would never wait for
the elevator, but race down the four flights two steps at a
time. I could never wait to get back.

   - Perhaps something other than Central
   Park prompted your returning to PH-F
   earlier than 5:00 p.m. when, by your own
   admission, Mr. Kalich, Broadway matinee
   performances normally break.

   - Like what?

   - Perhaps, when nobody answered the phone,
   you saw it as a last chance to put a halt
   to your cruel games before the Final Game
   was even played.

An extension has been added to the wrought-iron terrace fence to compensate for the space between it and the stone gargoyle from which the boy and girl leaped to their death. Still, if one is truly zealous, one could always climb from the wooden bench seated beneath the fence onto its edge and, teetering on the edge, and using the fence as ballast, take the final plunge. However, no trace of the previous space between the fence and the stone gargoyle exists today. Like the boy and girl, it's as if it was never there.

- As concierge on that ever fateful Sunday, Mr. Rivera, when Mr. Kalich returned from the park to see the shattered bodies of the boy and girl lying in front of the building: how did he act?

- What do you mean act?

- Did he act strange, for instance? Was he shocked? sad? surprised? remorseful?

The concierge doesn't respond.

- Did he seem as if he half expected it?

The concierge reflects.

- Fernando...er...Mr. Rivera, how did he act?

- It's hard to explain.

- Why is it hard to explain?

- Because Mr. Kalich didn't act at all.

Though I still have memories of Dobrinka standing on the wooden bench in front of just that space and, knowing my fear of height, teasing me by raising her arms as if to take the plunge herself. And how instantly I would rush to put my arms around her and hold her tight to protect her.

- Mr. Kalich, Officer Connelly has reported that your video camera was positioned at such an angle that the boy and girl's suicide leap could have been recorded.

- Yes. I forgot to mention that.

- You forgot to mention that?!

- Also, when Officer Connelly first entered your apartment, Mr. Kalich, he maintains you were watching your TV monitor.

- That's likely.

- The officer further asserts that nothing was showing on the screen other than snowflakes.

- Sometimes snowflakes are all there is.

POSSIBLE ENDINGS FOR NOVEL: TRANSFIGURATION OF THE COMMONPLACE	POSSIBLE ENDINGS FOR NOVEL: PENTHOUSE F
a) Novel as basis for a reality TV program.	a) Novel as basis for a reality TV program.
b) Robert Haberman sitting in front of his blank TV screen.	b) Richard Kalich sitting in front of his blank TV screen.
c) Show Haberman initiating the Selection Process for a new boy and girl.	c) Show Kalich initiating the Selection Process for a new boy and girl.
d) Show Haberman commencing to write novel, "Transfiguration of the Commonplace," from his aborted novel's notebook.	d) Show Kalich commencing to write novel, "Penthouse F," by assembling pages he's already written by having lived the experience.
e) Leave Reader uncertain as to whether Haberman's perceptions of the boy and girl are real or imagined.	e) Leave Reader uncertain as to whether the book is reality-based or fiction.

- Mr. Kalich, it's my understanding that you have already commenced writing your new novel.

- I wouldn't call it writing.

- What would you call it?

- Assembling pages. To be precise, the novel, Penthouse F, in a sense has already been written as it's coincident on my having lived the experience with the boy and girl.

- So you no longer suffer from writer's block?

- No, of course not. That was the whole point in my having lived the experience with the boy and girl, was it not? For the first time in my life I am truly able to take dictation.

In the dressing room when I challenged Dobrinka to choose between the actor and myself, citing it as a moment of truth, did I really believe my words or was I again, as always, merely taking dictation?

- Mr. Kalich, you make it sound as if the entire experience with the boy and girl, from its very inception to the end, was just so much grist for your writer's mill.

- I was under the impression that we already established that much.

…

- If I could have written the novel "Transfiguration of the Commonplace" when I first envisioned it, everything would have been different.

- You mean to say Penthouse F would never have been written.

- I mean to say Penthouse F would never have been lived.

- MR. KALICH, MR. KALICH, I WANT YOU TO TAKE WHAT I SAY SERIOUSLY...

- AND NOT SERIOUSLY AT ALL.

Some comments on Kalich's previous novel, *Charlie P*:

"*Charlie P* is energetic, delightfully sardonic, dark without being oppressive, playful and very readable."
—Sven Birkets

"*Charlie P* seems to me unlike anything in American literature. There's a remarkable lightness to it, a beauty in its willingness to blur the line between reality and fantasy...." —Brian Evenson

"Charlie P an idiot, in the noblest sense of that term, a schlemiel, a beautiful loser, a benighted hero, a virtuoso of the otiose." —Warren Motte

"This is an intriguing psychic landscape. Kalich successfully reproduces the sensation of existential indecision and doubt in all its intensity." —Stacey Levine, *American Book Review*

Charlie P is available from Green Integer.